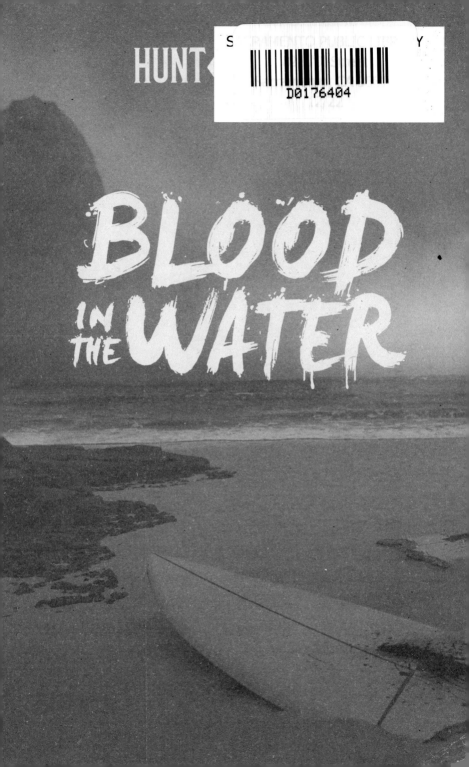

# HUNT A KILLER®

# *BLOOD* IN THE *WATER*

## AN ORIGINAL NOVEL BY CALEB ROEHRIG

SCHOLASTIC INC.

Copyright © 2022 by Gnomish Hat Inc.

ISBN 978-1-338-78403-9

10 9 8 7 6 5 4 3 2 1          22 23 24 25 26

Printed in the U.S.A.          40

First printing 2022

Book design by Katie Fitch and Jessica Meltzer

Photos ©: vi: Evgenia_art/Getty Images; 125 foreground: Raggedstone/Alamy Stock Photo; 187 icon: CSA-Archive/Getty Images; 237 top background: EyeEm/ Alamy Stock Photo; 237 bottom background: onurdongel/Getty Images; 237 crates: Liudmila Chernetska/Getty Images. All other photos © Shutterstock.com

# BEACHCOMBER

## STARTERS

| | |
|---|---|
| BASKET OF FRIES | $2.99 |
| FRIED OYSTERS | $8.99 |
| LITTLENECK CLAMS | $12.99 |
| PEEL & EAT SHRIMP | $10.99 |
| CRAB DIP | $5.99 |

## SOUPS & SALADS

| | |
|---|---|
| GARDEN SALAD | $3.49 |
| SEAFOOD SALAD | $6.99 |
| GAZPACHO | Cup: $3.99 Bowl: $5.99 |
| NEW ENGLAND CLAM CHOWDER | Cup: $4.99 Bowl: $6.99 |

## ENTRÉES

| | |
|---|---|
| HAMBURGER | $10.99 Add cheese: 50¢ |
| CRAB CAKES | $11.99 |
| FISH 'N' CHIPS | $12.99 |
| TIGER PRAWNS | $10.99 |
| GRILLED SEA BASS | $14.99 |
| CATCH OF THE DAY | MARKET PRICE Grilled or fried |

## SIDES

| | |
|---|---|
| FRENCH FRIES | $1.99 |
| ONION RINGS | $2.99 |
| POPCORN SHRIMP | $3.49 |

# ONE

The biggest downside to working on the beach is all the tourists who say things like *You must love getting to work on the beach*. Especially when I'm standing in front of them just barely holding on to a plastic tub stacked with dirty dishes, used napkins, and half-eaten food. People spill beer on me, yell at me, and don't tip—and the closest I get to the ocean is the few miserable yards of sand that make up our outdoor seating area—but yeah, sure. I'm really *living the dream*.

Tonight, the culprits are a group of girls huddled together under one of the heat lamps set up on the patio, all of them shivering in T-shirts and halter tops, despite the fact that temperatures are still dipping well into the fifties at night here. They're Spring Breakers, though—you could clock them a mile away—and they're going to wring every second of fun out of this sweet, sweet beach life until it gives them hypothermia.

Spring Breakers, ironically enough, are both the second-biggest downside as well as the biggest *upside* to working on the beach. They're loud and obnoxious, they get drunk and start fights, and they wreck things for the sole purpose of recording themselves doing it and then going viral on social media; they barf in the sand, they treat locals like their personal staff . . . and did I mention they spill beer on me? Because they do that *a lot*.

But if they stopped coming, the restaurant would fold in about a week—and then the entire rest of the town would follow. So you can't live with 'em . . . but you sure as hell can't live without 'em. At least, not in Barton Beach.

The fact is that this isn't such a bad place to live, most of the year; there's the occasional burglary, and something of a drug problem, but otherwise the crime rate is low and things are . . . sleepy. The quintessential postage-stamp town, it's barely two square miles in area—and aside from the pier, the boardwalk, and about a half mile of pictur-esque, oceanfront sand, we don't have much. Townies like me and my family depend on the business the high season brings in to keep us afloat for the rest of the year.

So when some drunk frat bro accidentally dumps his drink on me and forgets to apologize, I just tell him, "Forget about it," and reward my superhuman restraint by transferring five bucks of my meager tip earnings into my college fund. I've invested a hundred dollars so far this year alone, and it's not even April yet.

"Zac—a two-top and a four-top just opened in the garden, and I need those tables cleared, like, *now*." Haley Jensen gets in my way, her hands on her hips, affecting her best Night-Shift Manager tone. Which is hilarious, since she's (a) the hostess, (b) a seasonal hire, and (c) barely older than me. "The wait list is ridiculous, okay? I've got people backed up halfway to the boardwalk!"

"So, tell them to buy some saltwater taffy. It'll curb their appetites," I grumble under my breath. Before she can ask me to repeat myself, I jostle the bone-crushing tub of dishes. "I have to get these to the kitchen first, but I'll take care of those tables next."

"Some of these people have been waiting for almost an hour already!" she exclaims, tossing her hands out. "Do you have any idea what it's like out there? You know, maybe I should tell your dad he needs to hire more busboys, since apparently there aren't enough of you to get the actual job done."

"Sure thing, Haley." Shoving past her and heading for the kitchen, I plaster an insincere smile across my face. "You do that."

Typical of a conversation with Haley, it barely lasted thirty seconds, and already I can feel a migraine coming on. My dad will never hire another busboy when he's got me to do the job for free, and she knows it; she's just threatening to tattle, because she wants to put me in my place.

Which, I guess, brings me to the *third*-biggest downside of working on the beach: having my dad as my boss. The Beachcomber isn't very big, just a half-dozen indoor tables, a dozen more in the outdoor "garden" area, and then a patio set aside for the bar crowd. The menu is the standard grease-bomb burgers and seafood dishes you'd expect from a cozy little shack with an ocean view, but it was founded by my grandfather, so my dad thinks it's the most important restaurant in town.

Well, I guess from a practical standpoint, it *is*—at least where the Fremont family is concerned. Although we're not very big, either.

"I heard Haley shouting at you," my little sister, Ruby, comments the second I enter the kitchen. There's a table set up in the corner near the door where she gets to hang out on nights our dad can't find anyone to stay with her, and she's got her eyes locked on her tablet computer. "Tell her that if she complains about you to Dad, you'll tell him how she lied about being sick last weekend so she could go to Atlantic City with her boyfriend."

I pause as I'm unloading the dishes. "Is that true? Actually, wait—don't tell me. If you hacked into her email or something, it'll make me an accessory after the fact."

"Didn't need to. She tweeted from a casino with her location on." Ruby chews her thumb absentmindedly, still not looking up from her tablet. "Not exactly a criminal mastermind. Of course, if she really wanted to get away with it, she wouldn't have brought her phone with her at all—it's a total amateur move. All you'd need to do is check the GPS tracking on her cell to show she was lying when she said she was home with the flu."

"I don't think Dad has the kind of resources to triangulate people's cell phones, or whatever." I smile at the thought, though—Haley Jensen on the witness stand, frantic, caught in her lies. "Especially since we don't actually require doctor's notes for sick days."

"I'm just saying." Finally, Ruby spares me a glance. "That's how they caught the Falls Church Hatchet Killer. He chopped his whole family into pieces—*pieces*, Zac!— while pretending to be in Richmond on a business trip, but his phone records showed he'd driven back to town that same day, and he was busted. I learned about it on the *Behind True Crime* podcast."

My headache/brain tumor gets worse, and I groan. "Come on, Ruby, you're twelve! You're too young for that stuff. It's gonna give you nightmares."

"You know what gives me nightmares? *Health-code violations*." She mouths the last three words, gesturing above my head—to where an elliptical rack of pots and pans hangs from the ceiling by a literal thread. It started to collapse two years ago when dry rot buckled one of the ceiling joists it's bolted to, and now it's mostly held in place by a rudimentary rope and pulley. "Leave my podcasts alone. At least they're about actual historical events—and they almost always end with the bad guy getting caught! Or at least identified. Before he disappears forever with lots of money and a bloody hatchet."

Her expression barely changes, and I start to think she's spending way too much time in this kitchen, surrounded by adults who say whatever they want because they've forgotten there's a kid present. "Do I need to tell Dad what kind of stuff you're listening to?"

"Do I need to tell him you're not clearing tables fast enough?" she counters instantly.

"Touché." I roll my eyes, hoisting my now-empty tub and starting for the garden. "You're a monster, Ruby Roo."

"Mess with me, you get the horns!" she calls as the door swings shut behind me.

———

When I say that I work on the beach, I mean that I literally work *on the beach*. Our family restaurant is one of only a handful of businesses that sit right on the actual sand itself, in the shadow of the boardwalk, with the ocean gradually eating away at our front yard. We call the outdoor seating area the "garden," because that's what Grandpa called it, for whatever reason, but in reality, it's just a cluster of tables arranged in close enough proximity to the bar that we can still serve alcohol to the people who sit out there.

Okay, I guess I mean the royal "we" here, because I'm only sixteen and I'm not allowed to serve alcohol to anyone. Hence the reason I'm a free busboy instead of a free waiter. But it's a family business, and Dad says he wants us all to think of everything as "ours," which is only risky when you put Ruby too close to the maraschino cherries.

The surf is up tonight, the Atlantic slapping loudly against the shore as I clear the two-top and four-top that had Haley so deep in her feelings, and I take a moment to look out at the water. It's a pretty impressive sight. White-caps froth in the moonlight as they surge against the beach, and the pier—lit up like a bandstand directly across from us—casts dazzling reflections over the choppy waves. From here, you can just see the beacon at the end of the jetty that marks the start of Dead Man's Cove. It's flashing, I realize, and the way the air smells makes me wonder if our busy night will be cut short.

"Seems like it's gonna rain, doesn't it?" As if reading my mind, Mia Montes sidles up to me while I'm stacking the last of the grimy plates in my grimier tub, her expression defeated.

"I think my dad fixed the awning," I say eagerly—*too* eagerly, like embarrassingly eagerly—pointing at the mechanical apparatus that's currently ratcheted up against the front of the building. It broke last winter, and it went on the long list of Things to Deal With . . . somewhere ahead of the collapsing kitchen rack but behind the escalating property taxes. "Look at the bright side: If the weather goes to crap, people won't want to leave!"

"Yeah, but if they don't order more food, I don't get any more tips." Mia sighs, running a hand through her dark hair, and I try not to make any pathetic whimpering or groaning noises out loud.

Mia might honestly be the most gorgeous person on the planet. A student at the community college in the nearby city of Franklin Harbor, she's one of the Beachcomber's precious few year-round employees not named Fremont. She started out as a seasonal hire two summers ago, and then just never quit—and even though she's nineteen, and she's told me several times that she's too old for me, I'm holding out hope that she'll eventually change her mind.

"We can take Haley's tips," I suggest. "I'll hold her while you kick her shins?"

"Better have Ruby do the kicking." Mia grins, dimples appearing in her cheeks, and my stomach flips over. "At least she's intimidating. The other day, she told me some methods for disposing of human remains that I . . . don't think I'll ever be able to forget. No offense, but there's something kinda freaky about a twelve-year-old who memorizes that stuff. I mean, it's more of a Dana Scully way than a Dexter way, but still."

"She's got this fixation with true-crime stuff." I shake my head, not sure what to do about Ruby's latest obsession. She's always seemed mature for her age, but she's only twelve, and it's hard to know if she really takes stuff in stride as much as she seems to. "Have you seen my dad, by the way? Haley got on my case earlier, and I should probably do a preemptive strike, before she gets the chance to tell him what a slacker I am."

Mia shrugs. "Last I heard, he was meeting with someone in his office."

With my tub once again full of dirty dishes, I trudge back to the kitchen—an endless cycle I repeat pretty much every single day during the high season—and once I've unloaded the tub for the umpteenth time, I go looking for my dad. His office is behind the bar, so I start in that direction, but I stop when I nearly run right into him outside the kitchen door.

"Thanks for letting me take up your time, Luke." The man standing with my dad shoots the cuffs on a gaudy, button-down shirt, and I turn around immediately, pretending to organize a basket of soup crackers while listening in. I want to make sure I don't lose track of Dad, of course—but if I'm honest, I'm also really curious about what they're saying. "I'm glad to know I can count on you. You're one of the good ones."

"Any time, Mr. Webb." Dad looks kind of moody and distracted, with dark circles under his eyes—but lately, that's not really unusual. Every year it gets a little more expensive to run the restaurant, but we basically maintain the same number of customers. "You know how I feel about protecting small businesses in Barton Beach. We're part of what makes this community special, and I'm happy to do what it takes to see that things stay that way."

"Good man." Vincent Webb thumps my dad on the shoulder and gives him the wide, empty smile of a Realtor who's glad you didn't check the basement.

It's a little weird to see Vincent Webb, the wealthiest man in town and owner of half the businesses on the board-walk, at the Beachcomber. Having started out with nothing, he's a man who makes a point of flaunting his newfound wealth. He wears designer shirts, luxury sunglasses, and Italian loafers—but it's all ugly as sin. He's the kind of guy who sorts the price from high to low and then buys what-ever comes up first, because the whole point is showing off how much he can afford to spend. Meanwhile . . . well, we buy off-brand ketchup in bulk and then pour it into the nicer bottles and hope nobody can tell the difference. If he needed to see my dad badly enough to slum it with us down on the beach, there must be a good reason.

"I'll get back to you with details about the city council meeting, but I think we ought to organize a town hall, too. We can rustle up some average-Joe types to voice their concerns." Webb scans the dining room, and for once, I'm glad it's so crowded. It's not as clean as it should be, and he's a guy who notices that sort of thing, but at least he'll see that the Beachcomber is popular. "Your brother around tonight? He and Paige might be just who we need to get some more of the locals on board."

"Flash?" Dad snorts a sarcastic laugh. "It would be nice if he'd actually take an interest in the family business once in a while, but no—he's not here, and I wouldn't count on him helping us out."

Webb's eyebrows go up a little. "Really? Isn't he part owner of this place?"

"In name only." Dad doesn't mince words, and his tone is so blunt I actually wince a little. The restaurant is small enough that there are plenty of tables within earshot of their conversation, and this feels like laundry that shouldn't be aired quite so publicly. "He's not big on obligations or responsibilities."

"Well." Webb shifts, looking almost as uncomfortable as I feel. "I'd still like to get him involved, if we can . . . Flash Fremont is something of a hero to this town, and he'd be useful to have in our corner. Where's he hanging out these days?"

"Probably on the beach." Dad shrugs, uninterested. "But I don't really know—and I wouldn't hold my breath if I were you. Counting on Flash Fremont is a mistake. The only thing he does reliably is let people down." His face looks flushed in a way I recognize as the suppressed desire to smash something, and he adds, "The day my brother does something to benefit this restaurant instead of himself will be the day he dies."

With that, Dad bids Vincent Webb goodbye, and then he turns on his heel, stalking back to his office while the suddenly quiet dining room stares after him.

# TWO

"Dad? What was all that about?" When I catch up with him in his office a couple minutes later, I'm almost afraid to ask. It's not like him to air personal business in public like that. "Is everything . . . okay?"

It's not much of a question, but I've got no idea how to ask what I really want to ask. *What's his problem with Uncle Flash?* Pinching the bridge of his nose, Dad gestures at the desktop in front of him, cluttered with paperwork. "No, it is definitely not okay. The price of sea bass is up, one of our fryers is on its last legs, and they're predicting a cold snap for next week—just in time to chase people off the beach."

"No, I meant, like . . . why was Vincent Webb here?"

"Oh, yeah—more good news." He slumps in his ancient swivel chair, springs creaking, and ages ten years before my very eyes. "The city council wants to rezone some land around the boardwalk, because some hotel chain wants to build a damn resort here—which would level the competition, raise rents and taxes through the roof, and put pretty much all of us out of business. Vincent is trying to organize against it, and he came to see if we'd back him up."

"*He* needs *us* for backup?" I try not to sound skeptical, but . . . "I mean, he's, like, the richest man in Barton Beach. He practically owns the boardwalk! Wouldn't a resort mean a whole lot more rich people buying souvenirs and eating at Whitecaps?"

Located at the very end of the pier, Whitecaps is *the* premier dining experience in town: floor-to-ceiling windows looking out at the Atlantic Ocean, ten-page menus that come in those little leather folders, and ketchup that's served in brushed-steel ramekins so guests will wonder if maybe it was made from scratch. My best friend, Xavier, just started as a busboy there two weeks ago—and, I'd like to point out, *he* actually gets paid.

"There's more to life than turning a profit, Zac." Dad scowls at me. Just like that, he's back in his familiar form. "A resort-style hotel would completely change the landscape of Barton Beach and turn a unique destination into just another cookie-cutter tourist trap, like a hundred other places along the Eastern Seaboard. Vincent understands that." Then, with a grim little laugh, he says, "Not to mention that a resort would come with its own high-end restaurant that might actually steal business from Whitecaps."

He starts making a half-hearted attempt at sorting through the junk on his desk, and I realize he's not going to address the other half of his conversation with Webb if I don't remind him. "Why are you so mad at Uncle Flash?"

Dad glances up at me, his jaw shifting. "Forget about it. He draws an income from the Beachcomber but doesn't lift a finger to help out, and sometimes I just . . . It really ticks me off, you know?" He rubs his eyes, and his expression softens again. "Look, I know how much you admire him, but he's basically a deadbeat. He cadges off people, he sells crap on the beach . . . he can be really selfish. It's not easy being his big brother."

It makes me think of Ruby, and how she's probably more of an adult than I am, despite being four years younger than me. I keep worrying about what's influencing her, but it's never really occurred to me that *I* might be influencing her. "Can I help with anything? I mean, I can't fix the fryer or lower the price of sea bass, but maybe I could burn down some of the other bars so there's fewer places for Spring Breakers to go during the cold snap?"

This gets a laugh out of him at last. "You can go clear off some more tables so I don't have Haley in here for the third night in a row, telling me I need to replace you with her boyfriend."

"They were in Atlantic City last weekend." I blurt it before I can even give it a second thought—and I must say, it turns out confession *is* good for the soul. "She tweeted from a casino with her location on."

Dad laughs again. "Just get back to work, hotshot."

━━━━━━

I shut the door behind me, but I don't even make it five feet before I've walked headfirst into my third or fourth crisis of the evening. A very muscular—and evidently very drunk— man is getting in the bartender's face, while Mia does her best to intervene, trying to talk the guy down.

"Come on, Shotgun, let's go outside. There's supposed to be a storm later, so this is a good time to get a little fresh air," she says soothingly.

"I don't want no fresh air—I want the beer I asked for!" Shrugging her off like a horse swatting at flies with its tail, Dustin "Shotgun" McInnes glares at the bartender. "This stuck-up little twerp's been taking my money all night, and now he thinks it's no good all of a sudden!"

"You've had too much to drink." The bartender, another seasonal hire, has turned the same color as those mara-schino cherries Ruby loves so much. "And I have not been taking your money 'all night'—my shift just started twenty minutes ago!"

"Then how d'you know I had too much to drink?" Shotgun slurs triumphantly, almost clobbering Mia when he swings his arms wide in emphasis.

"You've got a couple of tells, Shotgun," she mutters, but when she tugs him away from the bar this time, he stumbles with her easily enough. "Come on. That guy's a jerk, and he'd probably spit in your beer anyway."

"Yeah, he prolly would." Shotgun limps a little as Mia leads him to the exit, bumping into people and barstools as he goes by. "You guys oughtta fire him. Get someone who can tell the difference between VIPs and this spring-break trash."

"This is the third time this week that guy's been in here, getting wasted and picking fights," the bartender, whose name tag says KYLE, grouses the minute Shotgun is out of the room. "Do you have a blacklist? Can we put him on it?"

"We don't, and even if we did, we probably couldn't." Kyle also came up here from Franklin Harbor, but unlike Mia, he doesn't know anything about how the townies conduct their affairs. "Shotgun is . . . sort of a local celebrity? He and my uncle were both pro surfers for a while, and they were both kind of a big deal—like, internationally. People take that stuff really seriously in Barton Beach."

That's because surfing is to Barton Beach what football is to small towns in Texas and the Midwest, with the locals treating the most promising athletes like genuine royalty.

Things that happened on the water twenty or thirty or even forty years ago, so long as someone is around to remember them, get rehashed on a regular basis.

But Dad has no patience for it—especially where his brother is concerned. Like any Barton Beach kid, he surfed recreationally, but he was never as serious about it as Uncle Flash, and he always thought the whole celebrity aspect of it was ridiculous. The way people around here like to gossip about the ancient past is embarrassing, according to him, and that goes double for the myths and legends surrounding his kid brother.

Casting a glance across the crowded patio, to where moonlit water still crashes against the shore, I add, "Anyway, because of some bad blood between them from back then, my dad feels like we need to be cool with Shotgun. Snubbing him would be more trouble than it's worth."

"He's a drunk." Kyle's assessment is as flat and unsentimental as I'd expect from someone who didn't grow up here. "And, by the way, that 'bad blood' isn't as old as you think it is; every time that Shotgun dude is in here, he starts trash-talking your uncle, saying he wants to 'settle scores' with him. Whatever that means."

It means that this is Barton Beach, and the only things that ever change around here are the tides, the tourists, and the temporary staff. Otherwise, we all grow up in the same neighborhoods, go to the same schools, date the same people, work the same jobs, and nurse the same grudges—forever and ever, amen. My dad and I had the same teacher for freshman English, for Pete's sake.

The group of spring-break girls I encountered earlier barges up to the counter then, having finally retreated indoors from the plunging temperatures. As they begin to bark their orders, Kyle gives me a plaintive look. "Hey, man, do you think you could run to the freezer and grab some vanilla ice cream? I'm almost out, and the vodka root beer floats are all anybody seems to want tonight."

"Yeah, sure," I tell him, thinking I can now add "unpaid barback" to my job experience on future college applications—along with "unpaid dishwasher," "unpaid kitchen prep," and "unpaid babysitter."

Another two-top has opened in the dining room, and I make a mental note to come back for it as soon as I've delivered the ice cream, because I can already smell the brimstone from Haley's next temper tantrum hanging in the air. Picking up speed, I shove through the door to the walk-in freezer—and immediately trip over someone hunkered on the floor in front of one of the shelving units. It's only thanks to dumb luck and fast reflexes that I keep from slamming face-first into the rubber mat on the ground.

"Whoa, you okay, kid?"

"Yeah, I'm fine." I say it reflexively, my heart still racing from the close call, and it takes a half second for me to realize who I'm talking to. "Uncle Flash? What are you do—"

"Hey, keep it down, okay?" He glances over his shoulder at the closed door, which is so thick you could probably set off a firecracker in here without anyone hearing it. "Your dad and I aren't exactly best buddies right now, and I don't want him to know I stopped by."

"But what are you—" I freeze when he turns back around again, and I get a good look at his face in the light for the first time. Uncle Flash—technically Christopher "Flash" Fremont, although nobody ever uses his first name—is usually a pretty good-looking guy. He's in his late thirties, but he's still got that surfer-boy swagger: tall, rangy, and tanned from a life lived outdoors. Tonight, however, he looks *rough*. Pale and drawn, he's got a livid bruise forming around his left eye. "Dude, what happened to you?"

"It's nothing." He waves the question away with a brusque, irritated motion. "I just . . . I broke up a fight on the beach between a couple of junkies, and my face got in the way of their fists. It happens. No good deed goes unpunished, right?" He holds up a bag of frozen peas from the shelving unit and presses it to his face. "Anyway, I came in here looking for something to ice it."

For a second, I just stare at him, not sure what to make of this. "You know, we've got a whole machine behind the bar that just . . . makes ice. Like, the actual stuff, so you don't have to hold a side dish on your face."

"Yeah, and like I said, I don't need your dad seeing me and getting on my back," he returns churlishly. "I came in here because I didn't want to have to answer a hundred questions about me getting my clock cleaned by a couple of scrawny tweakers."

"Okay, well, sorry I asked." It's stupid, but my feelings are actually a little hurt. Flash has always been one of the coolest guys I know: athletic, suave, easygoing. It's not like him to be this touchy. If Dad's not acting like himself tonight, then neither is my uncle. "It's actually kind of funny that I ran into you—literally, even. Seems like nobody can keep your name out of their mouth tonight."

"Oh?"

"We just had to cut Shotgun off—the bartender says he's been coming in lately, getting drunk and talking about kicking your fill-in-the-blank." I laugh at the idea . . . but I guess the truth is that Shotgun McInnes is one of the few men who might actually be able to take my uncle in a fair fight. He's big enough and mean enough, anyway. "And Vincent Webb was here earlier, talking to Dad about some hotel thing. He thought you might be able to help him rally the troops or whatever."

"Webb?" Uncle Flash looks up at me. It's impossible to

read his expression behind the bag of frozen peas, but his voice sounds . . . wary. "What hotel thing? What are you talking about?"

"I don't know . . . He's trying to stop the city council from passing some law about hotels on the boardwalk, and he wanted you to go drum up support, or something. Anyway, he was asking where to find you."

"Well, do me a favor and don't tell him." Uncle Flash makes an emphatic gesture with his free hand. "In fact, don't tell anybody—not Webb, not your dad, not your sister, *definitely* not Shotgun. Hell, if Paige calls, don't even tell her. I'm not exactly in the mood to be found right now."

"You want me to lie to your girlfriend?" I lift my brows. "I mean, I'll do it, but . . . don't you and Paige kinda live together? How are you supposed to avoid her?"

"Let me figure that out." He sighs, and he sounds ancient. "She's not my biggest fan right now, either, and she's got an even better left hook than the dude who gave me this." Pointing at his burgeoning shiner, he adds, "When she gets good and mad, it's best to just stay out of her way. Trust me on this one, bud: Girls are nothing but trouble."

Thinking about Mia—the way her hair falls down her back, the way her dimples appear when she smiles, the way she smells when she shows up for work . . . like strawberries and vanilla—I just can't agree with my uncle. I've met

Paige and *she* is definitely trouble, but I think that's just his type.

"Are you sure you don't want me to get you some actual ice? I'm on my way back to the bar anyway."

"No, forget it." He chucks the frozen peas onto the shelf again and drags his fingers through his hair. "I shouldn't stick around. Sooner or later, somebody's gonna come in here who *will* tell your dad. I probably should've never come here in the first place."

"Well, I don't think anybody's seen you yet—except for me." I wrap my arms around myself, the chill of the freezer starting to dig into my bones. "And I promise I won't say anything."

"Thanks. Thanks, Zac." He looks genuinely relieved. "You're a good kid."

For a moment, I just watch him, and he's so preoccupied he doesn't even notice; he keeps glancing at the door every few seconds, his mouth tight, and his jaw working silently. He's fighting with Dad, avoiding his girlfriend, and basically hiding in a walk-in freezer . . . Obviously, something is going on with him, but it's equally clear that he doesn't want to talk about it. Rubbing the back of my neck, I say, "Are we still on for surfing this weekend?"

"Huh?" He looks up at me like I've started speaking Turkish.

"You said you'd take me out to Spivey Point if the waves were good," I remind him. Historically, Flash has been a fun uncle, if not a reliable one. He has a history of making promises and then forgetting them, but I've been begging him to show me Spivey Point—the world-class beach on the other side of Franklin Harbor where he won the Coastal Elites Surf Invitational the year I was born—since pretty much the day I first learned it existed. "We talked about it, like, two weeks ago?"

"Oh. Oh, yeah, of course." He nods, but by the way he says it, I can tell he doesn't remember. Instantly, my chest deflates a bit. I'd really been excited about that trip. "Look, Zac, I just got a lot going on right now, and . . ." Trailing off, Flash sighs, seeming to finally realize how full of it he sounds. "Okay, bud, I'll level with you: I forgot. I've been a pretty lousy uncle lately, and I know it. There's just . . . Something happened that I didn't anticipate, and dealing with it has kind of pushed everything else to the side. I get how that's not much of an excuse, but . . ."

I find myself nodding, because there really isn't any other way to respond. "I get it."

"I'm serious, bud. I know it's not cool, and I feel bad." He bumps my shoulder with his fist, conjuring up a familiar, roguish smile. "Don't let me hold you back, though. You've finally got what it takes to handle Spivey. You should go."

Of course I could go to Spivey Point alone, but the

whole reason I asked him was so we could ride those waves together. He taught me how to surf right here in Barton Beach, when I was a kid—showing me the basics, buying me my first board, helping me get a feel for the water. He took me to the qualifying heats for the longboard championship every year so I could watch pros at work. It's been our *thing*, our ritual. Going by myself just wouldn't be the same.

"Listen," he begins, squaring his shoulders and glancing around the walk-in freezer. "I hate to ask this, but I gotta get going, and . . . could you just check to make sure the coast is clear before I hit it?"

Glumly, I agree. Poking my head out of the freezer, I see that Ruby still has her attention on her tablet, and the rest of the kitchen staff are all occupied, so I signal to Uncle Flash and cover for him while he darts toward the rear exit, where we take the trash out to the dumpsters shared by all the oceanfront businesses.

Slipping through the door ahead of him, all I see is the short expanse of dark sand between the restaurant and the pilings of the elevated boardwalk. The sulfurous glare of overhead safety lamps cast eerie shadows at my feet, but otherwise it's deserted. The wind has picked up, and it carries the less-than-appealing scent combination of salt water, fried food, and rotting garbage that is a little too familiar to those of us who work *"on the beach."*

I wave Uncle Flash out after me, and when the door eases shut, we're alone again. The boardwalk stretches north to south, with wooden steps descending to the sand at irregular intervals, and all the business down here—us, a hot dog stand, an ice cream place, and a short-order fish fry—back right up against it. Along this makeshift corridor, he could probably walk at least a quarter mile without being seen by anyone.

"You're a lifesaver, bud." He wraps me in a hug, and for the first time, I realize just how badly *he* smells—like flop sweat and unwashed hair—and it makes me wonder again just exactly what's going on with him. What's got him run so ragged, hiding in the walk-in, avoiding the people he cares about?

Before I can ask, however, a large figure lurches suddenly around the rear corner of the Beachcomber, lumbering crookedly across the sand toward the pilings of the boardwalk. Habitually favoring one leg, his hair swinging in his face, it's Shotgun McInnes.

And when he sees my uncle, his bleary eyes snap into focus and his expression darkens with rage. Starting toward us, his meaty hands balling into fists, he spits, "Flash Fremont? Oh, I been waitin' for this. You're a dead man!"

# THREE

If a train left Kansas City heading east at eighty-five miles per hour, and a second train left St. Louis traveling west at seventy miles per hour, the spectacular collision in the middle might look something like what's about to happen right in front of me. My first instinct is to get between them and stop it—to back Shotgun off and maybe talk him down the way Mia did inside—but it only takes a couple of seconds to realize how pointless that would be. My only choice is to either stand between the trains when they hit or get out of the way.

I choose safety, and I stand by in shock while an inebriated, six-foot-four Sasquatch of a man launches himself at my uncle. They both go flying into the sand, rolling over, muscles bulging and teeth bared. In all the years I've been around, these two have traded blows maybe three times—usually when they've both had too much to drink and there was nowhere to get out of each other's way. But I've never seen this kind of concentrated fury before.

Shotgun manages to pin my uncle to the ground and starts raining blows down on him, with a sick, frightening sound. Within seconds, though, Flash kicks him off—literally, slamming his foot so hard into the other man's gut that he retches into the sand before collapsing . . . and then the tables are turned. There's a hideous crunching noise as my uncle slams his forehead into Shotgun's face, breaking his nose, sending blood everywhere.

Shouting at him, I try to get close, but they flip over again—feet and hands clashing aimlessly—and I have to dance out of the way before I take a fist to the jaw. And that's the sight that greets Mia an instant later, when she pops out from the back of the restaurant with a pair of overfilled trash bags: two grown men, bloodied and feral, swinging at each other in the moonlight while I make a pathetic attempt to intervene.

"What the hell?" Her eyes going wide, Mia tosses the trash bags to the ground and rushes forward, holding her hands out like a lion tamer who forgot her chair. "Stop! *Stop it*, both of you!"

Shotgun goes for an uppercut, but his left knee buckles

on him at the last second, and he howls in pain as he drops to the sand. Seizing the opportunity, I finally wrap my arms around my uncle, shoving him back while Mia gets in front of Shotgun, keeping him from lurching to his feet again.

"Get the hell off me!" Uncle Flash snarls, struggling against my grip, his whole body shaking with rage and adrenaline. I rode a mechanical bull once at the county fair, and it was just like this: clinging on for dear life and hoping that when you land it isn't on your head. *"Get off me."*

When he shoves me aside at last, nearly sending me to the ground myself, he leans over and spits blood into the sand at his feet. Shotgun gives a wet, throaty laugh from where he's finally pushing his way upright, towering over Mia as she plants herself in front of him. Sneering balefully, the man taunts, "Whassa matter, Fremont? You had enough already? Don't want your nephew to see you get your face rearranged?"

"Look who's talking, Shotgun." Flash grunts, gesturing at the man's swollen nose. "Let's go for round two, huh? Maybe I'll break your other leg tonight."

"You son of a—" Shotgun's face purples behind the slick of dark blood that streams down over his mouth and chin. He lurches forward again, but Mia braces her hands on his chest and his weak knee buckles in the sand a second time. "I'm gonna mess you up, Fremont! You keep laughing, I'm gonna send all those perfect teeth of yours straight down your throat, you hear me?"

"I hear you. Sounds like, *'Wah, wah, wah, I'm a washed-up drunk.'*" My uncle straightens his spine, pulling his hair back from his face. There's a fresh cut over his eyebrow, and his lip is starting to swell, but he glares down at the other man with pure contempt. "You're nothing, Shotgun. You never were. Just a second-rate poseur who couldn't hack it on the water and can't get over it. You're pathetic."

Shotgun lurches forward again, testing Mia's resistance, and his eyes are wild with hatred as he glares at Flash across the sand. "You think you're somebody special because of stuff you did twenty years ago, but you ain't. You're a liar and a cheat, and the day's comin' when you're gonna get what's yours."

"Maybe." Flash spits again, more blood darkening the sand. "But it won't be coming from you."

"We'll see about that." Shotgun wipes his face, and for a second, I think he might be about to knock Mia down and make another run at my uncle, but then he steps back, thrusting out his finger. "You're dead meat, Fremont. You understand? I'm done playing nice with you. One of these days, we're gonna finish this once and for all, and you're gonna be sorry you ever tangled with me. You get that? *You're dead!*"

With that, he finally wheels around, stalking away into

the darkness without a backward look—until he's just one hulking shadow among many.

———

The night doesn't get much better after that. Mia wants to tell my dad about the fight, and I have to beg her not to, since I promised my uncle I would make sure no one knew he was here; Haley yells at me three more times; I drop a stack of plates that will probably come out of my nonexistent salary; and then the storm finally hits. Lightning splits the sky, a torrent of icy rain slams down on the beach, and I get drenched when I try to crank open the awning for the garden—only to find out it *wasn't* fixed, after all.

The restaurant turns into a ghost town after that, only a handful of patrons lingering around to see if things will let up, and when it becomes clear that the storm is going to last the night, Dad finally announces that we're shutting the Beachcomber early. The seasonal staff all breathe a sigh of relief, eager to go home, but for the rest of us, it's a pretty grim closing. As miserable as they are, we need every single one of these madcap busy nights we get, and losing one feels like whistling past the graveyard.

———

There's nothing quite like a coastal storm—a real one, the kind that shakes the glass for hours and makes you understand why people once thought gods were responsible for thunder. It's elemental and terrifying and reminds you how small you are. Water starts seeping into the dry storage area, and Dad makes me take Ruby home while he stays behind to deal with it. The waves are really landing hard outside, sending foam high into the air, and I cross my fingers that the power doesn't go out. If the contents of the freezer spoil, we're screwed in more ways than I care to think about.

I don't know how long dealing with the leak takes Dad in the end, because I'm in bed by the time I hear the front door open and close, and I'm way too tired to open my eyes so I can check my phone. But he's wide awake and ready to go again first thing in the morning, when he's banging on my door and announcing that it's time to head back to the Beachcomber.

Oh, yeah, in case I didn't mention it: The fourth-biggest downside to working on the beach is that you don't get a spring break. Okay, I'm allowed a day off here and there, and Dad doesn't exactly chain me to the kitchen prep counter for the duration. But while my friends all plan trips out of town or just lazy days doing nothing, all I do is hope I don't pull a muscle unloading frozen cod from a truck at 9:00 a.m.

The surf is quiet when we get to the beach that morning, the sky a milky gray and the sand littered with flotsam cast up by the violent waves. I can just see people out on the jetty near the beacon, some of them wearing Day-Glo vests, and I get the impression that it's some kind of emergency response. Maybe there's a beached whale or an unmoored boat that was driven into the rocky shallows of Dead Man's Cove during the storm. It wouldn't be the first time.

I definitely notice a little extra water damage on the plaster over the grill when I carry boxes of crab, whitefish, and leeks to the walk-in, and the ceiling rack looks a little more precarious, but otherwise, the restaurant seems okay, and I breathe a sigh of relief. The truth is, there are days when I fantasize about the place caving in entirely—getting flattened by a hurricane or burned to a crisp overnight thanks to an electrical malfunction. In these imaginings, my dad collects the insurance money, we all have a stoic little farewell to the Fremont legacy in Barton Beach, and then we . . . you know, move on.

Because as much as this place means to our family, it is so exhausting to have to worry about water damage and power outages and how we're going to repair the fryer, when I also have to worry about midterms and college funds and learning to drive.

Ruby and I are doing prep work side by side—peeling carrots and chopping onions, respectively—when there's a commotion from the front of the restaurant. One of the cooks pokes his head out to see what's up, and when he comes back, his face has lost all its color. "It's the cops, man. Two deputies, and they're asking for your dad. Whatever it is, it can't be good."

Ruby and I make it to the dining room right when Dad comes out of his office, just as the two deputies—guys I vaguely recognize, since Barton Beach is small enough that *everyone* is vaguely recognizable, at a certain point—remove their hats. "Luke . . . Mr. Fremont. I hate to say this, but we're here with bad news. I'm afraid that a body washed up in Dead Man's Cove sometime this morning, and . . . well, we'll need to do a formal identification for procedural purposes, but . . ."

He trails off, his face going red, and my heart slows down, my chest so tight I can't breathe. My body starts to react before he's even finished saying it, because some part of me just *knows*. And when the first deputy can't seem to find his voice again, the second one steps in to finish the statement. "Luke, we're really sorry, but . . . it's your brother. Apparently, Flash was out in the water last night, and, well . . . he's dead."

# FOUR

*"No."*

I don't even realize the voice is mine until I've taken a step back, my face stinging like I've just been hit. And then, just as quickly, I go numb all over. The words echo in my thoughts over and over—*he's dead, he's dead, he's dead*—but they don't make any sense. It feels suddenly as if I'm in a different room and all of this is happening somewhere else, to *someone* else. It can't be about Flash. Not my uncle.

Ruby freezes up, her eyes going blank behind her glasses, and Dad . . . Dad just stands there, expressionless, his complexion slowly turning gray.

They keep talking, but the noise in my head crowds them out. *He's dead, he's dead, he's dead.* I just keep thinking about how Flash was supposed to take me to Spivey Point—how even though he forgot, even though it was one more promise he broke, he would have come through eventually. Even when he was never around, he was always *around* . . . always aware when he'd screwed up, and always willing to redeem himself. Always available, sooner or later. He missed my thirteenth birthday, and then surprised me two weeks later with a whole day of plans for just the two of us. The movies, the arcade on the pier, some surfing, my favorite burger joint for lunch.

How is he supposed to make up for Spivey Point if what they're saying is true?

"From the looks of things, it might've been an accident," the first deputy ventures, still red in the face, speaking to my dad's shoes. "Could be that he went out last night, thinking he could handle those big waves as the storm was tapering off, and got sucked into the cove. He wouldn't be the first."

"No." I shake my head. "No way. He would never have gone—"

"Zac," Dad interrupts me, his voice strangled.

"No!" I surprise myself by shouting it, and everyone looks at me—including the cooks and servers who have been slowly gathering at the back of the room to watch. "Flash would never go out there in weather like we had last night, and you all know it! Not even when it was 'tapering off' at, like, what? Four in the morning?"

Ruby starts crying, really softly, like she's trying not to, and it makes something wrench open in my chest. For a minute, the room swims in front of me, and I have to blink tears out of my eyes as Dad says, "Zac . . . just let them talk, okay? We don't even know what they found."

"Unfortunately, the . . . uh, the rocks did kind of a number on him." The second deputy remains steady, but he clearly wishes he could be anywhere else. "You know how the cove is, and when the waves are as rough as they were last night . . . well."

Everyone in the room flinches, because we *do* know. Dead Man's Cove didn't get its name because they ran out of other options. A curved inlet about a third of a mile long, where the surf shallows abruptly and the currents race, it's separated from the main beach by the jetty just south of us. The movement of the tides over hundreds of years has filled it with sharp rocks, old coral, and fragmented shells—as well as broken glass, rusting metal, and other trash people have tossed out to sea. If you get too close, you can be dragged under, and if you're lucky, all that will happen is you'll be flayed alive as you're smashed repeatedly against the ocean floor.

"It's not pretty," the deputy concludes. "We hate having

to ask this, but we'll eventually need someone to come down to the morgue and ID the body."

"So you don't even know if it's actually him?" I want to grab the guy and shake him. "You're just—"

"We know it's him, son," he cuts me off. "But he still has to be officially identified by a family member. That's the rule."

"I can . . ." Dad looks around like he, too, just found himself in a different room all of a sudden. "I can get my coat—"

"No need, not yet. We still . . ." He glances at the other deputy, and a furtive look passes between them. "We're still assessing the scene."

"Assessing the scene?" Ruby repeats, her eyes blotchy but suddenly alert. "That means you're investigating, right? But if you think it was a surfing accident, then . . ."

"They don't think it was an accident." I cross my arms over my chest, narrowing my eyes. "Flash knew those waters better than anyone. He wouldn't have taken his board out at night, alone, in the middle of a storm—and he definitely wouldn't have gone anywhere near Dead Man's Cove." Gesturing out the windows in the direction of the beach, I ask, "Did he have an ankle tether when you found him? Was he wearing his wet suit? Because it was freezing even before the storm hit!"

When they don't answer me right away, just trading

more uneasy looks between them, Dad furrows his brow. "Wait a minute . . . is he right? What aren't you telling us—what is there that you have to 'assess'?"

"Look . . ." The first deputy coughs into his fist. "We haven't ruled out the possibility of an accident of some sort—it happens a few times a year, at least, and sometimes it's the guys with the most experience who get too cocky and bite off more than they can chew." Before I can protest, he holds up his hand. "We have to consider it. But . . . well, the fact is that we got a witness who claims he saw people out on the jetty last night during the storm, and according to what he described, it sounds like there was some sort of a . . . struggle."

"A *struggle*?" If anything, Dad's face goes even more pale, his tone incredulous. "You can't be serious. You're not really suggesting that it—that he—"

"You're saying he was murdered." My sister almost imbues the word with a hushed reverence, and Dad glares at her in horror.

"*Ruby!*" Dad snaps, and then squeezes his eyes shut, trying to check his temper. "Your uncle was not murdered! He . . . he drowned—right?" The deputies look at him blankly and then shrug a little, unwilling or unready to confirm it. "He spent all his time on the beach. Maybe he drank too much, passed out, and . . ."

"Got pulled in when the tide shifted?" the first deputy

concludes. "It's possible. Lots of things are possible. And we gotta keep an open mind to all of them at this stage and make sure we don't leave any stones unturned."

"Like the possibility that the struggle on the jetty last night was related to what happened to Flash," the second deputy jumps right in, smooth as can be. "We're not saying it was for sure foul play, but we have to explore it. After all, your son here just got done telling us what fools we'd be to think it might've been an accident."

My face heats up as the attention in the room turns back to me, but I try not to let it show. "Your witness couldn't have seen much—the rain was coming down in sheets."

"No, he didn't. Just figures on the jetty, moving around erratically, like they were fighting. Couldn't be sure if it was two people, or three, or more."

"Sounds like he isn't sure about much of anything," Dad remarks bluntly, his mouth tightening into a flat line. "Is this not tragic enough that you need to come in here and start throwing around terrible suggestions before you have even the slightest idea what happened?"

"Sir, we know there's been a death, and that it's not yet been explained." The deputy spreads his hands. "We have questions, and we need you to be aware of them."

"It's ridiculous to suggest that my brother was . . . was murdered. Everyone in this town loves him—he's a local hero!"

"Shotgun," I blurt before I can think better of it, not sure why my father is leaving out this significant detail. Once again, every head in the room swivels my way. "Shotgun McInnes. He hated Uncle Flash."

"That's not . . ." Dad shakes his head. "Zac, don't spread rumors. Not about something this serious. I mean, they're saying that your uncle . . . they're saying he's dead, and you can't just toss people's names out like that! What happened between Shotgun and your uncle was a long time ago."

"It's not a rumor!" I remember what the bartender said—*that "bad blood" isn't as old as you think it is*—and I press the palms of my hands against my eyes. "And I'm not talking about a long time ago, I'm talking about last night. He was here, Dad. They both were."

"What?" Dad blinks, and he looks at me like he's never seen me before. "What are you talking about? No one knew where your uncle was last night. He wasn't answering his phone."

"He was here! Or he stopped by, anyway—I talked to him. He got hurt breaking up a fight on the beach, and he needed an ice pack."

What's weird is that the story sounded plausible when Flash told it to me in the walk-in, but now that I'm repeating it, with an audience of two sheriff's deputies and a scattering of doubtful kitchen staff, I'm finally realizing how much of it doesn't add up. Flash was avoiding Dad, he didn't want to be seen, or for anyone to know where he was . . . and yet he came to the Beachcomber in the middle of the evening rush for a bag of frozen peas? During one of our busiest weeks of the year?

Feeling the heat of self-conscious nerves, I blunder ahead. "Look, the point is that Shotgun's been coming by the Beachcomber a lot lately, drinking and talking about settling old scores and stuff. Last night, he got so wasted the bartender had to cut him off! But when Uncle Flash was leaving again, they ran into each other out back, and . . . I mean, it was ugly."

"Son, I understand that you're trying to be helpful," the first deputy says, verbally rolling his eyes at me. "But it's not exactly a secret around here that your uncle and Shotgun McInnes didn't get along. Hell, they've been rivals since they were . . . what, eighteen? Nineteen?"

"Earlier." The second deputy corrects his partner with conviction. "I was a freshman when they both entered the Rising Stars tournament down at Spivey Point, and Flash was only a couple years ahead of me at school. They were like cats and dogs from day one." He lets out a low whistle. "Man, I still remember the day Shotgun broke his leg. Nothing was ever the same after that."

Dad clears his throat, loudly, and the deputy turns pink, snapping his mouth shut.

"You need to listen to me!" I slam my hand down on one of the two-tops, and Ruby jumps. "I'm not talking about something that happened a hundred years ago when you were in high school—I'm talking about *last night*. Shotgun jumped him out back, okay? Right in front of me! They were whaling on each other, and I'm pretty sure Uncle Flash broke Shotgun's nose, because it was . . . I mean, it was really gross and there was a lot of blood."

*"What?"* Dad repeats, eyes bulging. "Zac, if you're making this up—"

"I'm not! Why would you even say that?" I demand, looking around the room, my face getting hotter . . . and all I see is people not quite meeting my eyes. "Look, you can ask Mia—she helped me pull them apart! They were doing some real damage to each other, and when Shotgun left, he said Uncle Flash was 'dead meat.' He said he'd be sorry, and that he was gonna get what was coming to him."

There's another silence, longer this time, and then Dad sighs. "Listen, Zac . . . you just don't understand the history those two have—had. They were always at each other's throats, even when they were your age, and things only became worse as they got older. But it's been years since they had anything new to fight about. I'd be shocked if they've spoken more than ten words to each other in the last eighteen months!"

"Your father's right, son." The second deputy nods solemnly. "If they did brawl last night, as you say, it wouldn't even be the first time for that. This is a small town, and sometimes men boil over. It doesn't necessarily mean anything."

"Doesn't *mean* anything?" I can't believe my ears. "Are you even listening? They were beating each other to a pulp right in front of me, and Shotgun threatened my uncle when he was leaving!"

"The man's got a temper on him, that's true," the deputy allows, still seeming unbothered. "But he's no killer. We've never had him downtown for anything more serious than a drunk and disorderly and . . . well, the like, over the years. Nothing violent. Besides, the both of them have made some pretty ugly threats toward each other in the past. It's never amounted to much more than a bloody nose."

*Until last night,* I want to scream at him. Nothing ever amounts to anything until it's too late—and they didn't see the hatred in Shotgun's eyes, the way my uncle taunted him; they didn't hear the man say, *You're dead,* like he was trying to manifest it.

"How can you say he's not a killer when you haven't even started looking into it yet?" I demand, glaring at them—all of them. "They were fighting last night, right here on the beach, and Shotgun said, 'We're gonna finish this.' And then, a few hours later, some guys are fighting on the jetty, and my uncle washes up on the beach, and you're telling me I shouldn't see a connection?"

"Because we know the guy, okay?" The first deputy is starting to get testy. "And we know his history with your uncle. We'll go have a talk with him about last night, but I promise you, kid: If he ever had any intention of hurting Flash, he'd have done it years ago."

"They *were* hurting each other!" I tell them again, but it's like slamming my head against a brick wall. "And Shotgun could still be responsible even if he didn't mean to kill my uncle. If they picked their fight up again out on the jetty, in the middle of the rain, Flash could have slipped or been knocked off balance, and—"

"You gotta let us do our jobs, son." The second deputy cuts me flat, and my face is hot enough to replace our faulty deep fryer. "Besides," he adds, sharing yet another awkward glance with his partner, "Shotgun wasn't the only guy in town who might've had an ax to grind with your uncle."

"What does that mean?" Dad asks with an uneasy frown. "He didn't have any enemies in Barton Beach—this town acts like he hung the moon, for crying out loud."

The deputy fixes him with a cold expression and states, "I understand you got into a pretty nasty fight with Flash yourself just recently."

Dad goes rigid, and his throat bobs up and down. "That's . . . what are you getting at? Where did you hear that?"

"Half the department heard it, Luke." The first deputy sounds almost apologetic. "You two got into a shouting match two weeks ago right outside O'Malley's Pub. So many off-duty uniforms hang out there every day, you might as well have come down to the station and cursed each other out in front of the sheriff herself!"

"From what we hear, your exchange was . . . pretty heated." The second deputy folds his hands together and cocks a brow. "You want to tell us what it was about?"

The silence that follows is so loud it hurts my ears, Dad's hands closing into fists until cords of muscle bunch up in his forearms. When he doesn't say anything, when he doesn't tell them how off base they are, I start to get nervous. "Dad?"

"I've got nothing to say about that," he finally spits, quivering with rage. "How dare you come in here, telling me my brother is dead and then insinuating that I had something to do with it! How dare you?" Thrusting his finger at the door, he snarls, "Get out of my restaurant."

"Telling us off isn't gonna make this go away." The deputy keeps his voice level. "You're gonna have to answer our questions sooner or later."

*"Get out!"* Dad thunders, his eyes flashing, and Ruby starts to cry again. "The both of you can go to hell!"

With another wordless look, the deputies finally turn to leave, but at the door, the second man glances back. "We'll be in touch, Luke. Count on it."

It's not a promise that they'll follow up; it's a threat.

# FIVE

Dad doesn't speak to either of us after that; he just storms back to his office and slams the door, leaving me and Ruby to make sense of it all on our own. But what sense is there to make? *Uncle Flash is dead.* It just doesn't seem possible—like punching a hole in the sun, or something—and I keep repeating it to myself, trying to make it feel real. And the cops suspect our *dad?* If this is a nightmare, I'm more than ready to wake up.

Ruby cries for a long time, but that quiet, sniffly kind of crying—while I just struggle to wrap my brain around the fact that our uncle might have been *murdered.* It's stupid, but I keep thinking about how alive he was when he was here the night before. How I missed my chance to tell him how much he meant to me, because I was too busy guilt-tripping him for forgetting about the Spivey Point trip. Every few minutes, I turn and stare at the back door, thinking about how it was the last place I ever saw him.

The first person I text once I finally realize that I'm going to have to start telling people what's going on is my best friend, Xavier Hughes. He and I have been tight since elementary school, and in a lot of ways, Flash was like a surrogate uncle to him, too—teaching us both how to surf, taking us camping, answering the questions our parents didn't want us to ask. If anyone can help me understand how any of this is possible, it's him.

Fifteen minutes later, he's sitting with us in the kitchen, the three of us gathered around the prep table. Dad left at some point, still not saying a word to anyone, and I'm not even sure if the restaurant is going to open today. But I do know that we can hardly afford a second night of lost business, so we're all hacking our way robotically through a mountain of potatoes while Xavier does his best to keep Ruby and me company.

"Dude, they can't seriously think it was your dad," he says in a low voice, his eyes darting to the grill—where Eddie and Juan, the cooks, are almost certainly having their own sotto voce conversation about the same thing. "Luke 'Sweater Vests' Fremont? A killer?"

"It's always the ones you least suspect." Ruby is still subdued, speaking with this nearly monotone affect, in a totally creepy, horror-movie-twins kind of way. "Except for the Falls Church Hatchet Killer. He was pretty obvious."

"Ruby, quit saying stuff like that." I'm at the end of my rope, slicing potatoes while crime scene workers are probably zipping my uncle up in a black bag. My stomach turns over.

"They said Dad and Uncle Flash got into a big fight, but no one's told us what it was about," Ruby tells Xavier.

"It was probably about the restaurant." My hands are shaking, and I almost take the skin off my thumb with the knife. "When it comes to Dad, it's always about the restaurant."

I haven't told anyone about the conversation I had with him last night—how pissed he was at Flash for not pulling his weight, and the things he said to Vincent Webb in the middle of the dining room. *The day my brother does something to benefit this restaurant will be the day he dies.* It's bad enough to think about, let alone say aloud . . . and what if somebody gives that information to the cops?

What if they ask me what time Dad came home last night, and I have to say, *I have no idea, because it was so late I was already in bed?*

"It still could've been an accident," Xavier suggests in an unconvincing manner. He's had his fade refreshed recently—I can tell because he keeps rubbing the bare skin at the base of his neck to feel the stubble coming in. "They said they couldn't rule it out, right? I mean, who knows what that witness really saw?"

"They can't rule anything out yet." Ruby is still emotionless, still factual. "They'll have to do an autopsy just to officially figure out the cause of death. That's how it's done in cases like this."

"Stop saying 'cases like this'!" I slam my fist on the table hard enough to make both Ruby and the potatoes jump— and then I feel like a monster. "I'm sorry. I'm not . . . this isn't a 'case,' okay? It's Uncle Flash. It's *Dad*. What are we gonna do if they . . . if they arrest him?"

There's a silence after that, and Ruby's face goes from gray to alabaster. Finally, Xavier clears his throat. "He won't get arrested, dude. There's just no way your dad would do something like that. So they had a fight, or whatever—big deal! I fight with my sister all the time, and she's still alive. Unfortunately."

"It was Shotgun." I know the deputies wouldn't listen to me, but they're part of the same surf-groupie culture that runs Barton Beach. Shotgun McInnes might be a washed-up drunk these days, but to them he'll still be five international trophies and a dozen "Hometown Boy Does Good" headlines. "If you'd been there last night, you'd know I'm right. They weren't just swinging at each other to blow off steam—Shotgun was trying to put Uncle Flash in the hospital; you could see it in his eyes. Mia will back me up."

"But why?" Xavier asks. And, off my look, he hastens to add, "I just mean, like, what made him snap? They've been enemies forever, and Shotgun tells anyone who listens that Flash is the reason his leg was—"

"His ego was the reason. Everybody knows that," I state, giving him a withering look. The injury that resulted in Shotgun's limp is a subject we don't talk about around here. "Shotgun was careless, he got too close to the cove, and the currents pulled him under. He was lucky he hit the jetty instead of the rocks."

The incident happened the year after I was born, and it's one of the main examples that always gets brought up when we talk about water safety in Barton Beach. During a qualifying heat for the Regional Longboard Championship, on a day when the waves around the cove were especially epic, Shotgun fell off his board while trying to grandstand. He shattered his leg against the jetty, effectively ending his surfing career.

"He tried to blame Flash for the accident because he was jealous and he wanted to ruin his reputation." It almost worked, too; Flash ended up withdrawing from the championship just to prove it didn't matter to him—to shake off the rumors Shotgun was spreading—but some people believed the story anyway. "Look, the whole point is that, true or not, Shotgun has never let go of it. When he couldn't win any more competitions, his whole purpose in life became trying to tear down our uncle."

"I get all that." Xavier doesn't look at me, and I can tell he's holding in some sort of disagreement.

Annoyed, I add, "And maybe he didn't 'snap,' or whatever. Maybe he just did exactly what he said he was gonna do, and 'finish' it once and for all!"

"Sure, yeah." Xavier still sounds like he's trying to placate someone who's completely lost it . . . which honestly makes me feel like *I'm* about to lose it. "Could be he cornered Flash on the jetty and just picked up where they left off, but . . . I mean, it was coming down cats and dogs last night, man. That rain was *biblical*. With his bad leg, do you really think Shotgun could have kept his footing out there?"

"He has a limp—it's not like they replaced it with a wooden peg!"

"I think I know why Shotgun might have snapped." Ruby speaks up so suddenly it makes the knife leap from my hand. I didn't even notice when she slipped away from the table to fetch her tablet, but she's got it in her hands now, and she turns the screen to show us what she's found—an old article from the *Barton Beach Gazette*'s digital archive. Their back issues are supposed to be behind a paywall, but I've learned that my sister has tricks it's better I don't ask about.

# BLOOD IN THE WATER

**MARCH 24, 2007**

S. D. Malone

The latest round of qualifying heats for the Regional Longboard Championship ended in disaster yesterday afternoon, when a surfer collided with the stone jetty near Dead Man's Cove. The man has been identified as Dustin "Shotgun" McInnes, 23, a decorated athlete and Barton Beach local, who had been considered a front-runner in the upcoming tournament.

"It was awful," said one witness, a college student in town for spring break. "He was catching these really big waves near the beacon, and then . . . I mean, the next thing you know, he was under. And then the blood . . . I've never seen so much blood. We thought he was dead."

At the time of this printing, McInnes had not yet regained consciousness and was in critical care at Franklin Harbor General. According to his attending physician, he suffered a concussion and multiple broken bones.

"Tell you the truth, he's lucky," said Jamal Hughes, one of the Barton Beach lifeguards who pulled McInnes from the water. "Going under that close to the cove? Not a lot of people live to tell that tale. If the jetty hadn't stopped him, he'd have drowned, for sure."

Dead Man's Cove, the picturesque inlet at the south end of Barton Beach, is notorious for its fast currents and rocky shallows. Tourists and Beachers alike have been caught in its aggressive undertow over the years, and a proposal to dredge the land on that side of the jetty and fill it completely has been a standing item on the city council's agenda since 1972.

Jeremy Deacon, a representative for the Regional Longboard Championship, said in an official statement, "Our organization is committed not just to promoting the great sport of surfing, but to protecting the health and safety of our participating athletes. All heats are overseen by our judges, who do their best to prevent reckless behavior on the water, but the ocean is a wild place and accidents do happen. We offer our deepest sympathies to Mr. McInnes and his family."

But at least one witness, who declined to be named for publication, disputes the official characterization of the collision as an accident.

"There was another surfer boxing him in," the man stated in an interview with our reporter. "Dude with blond hair and blue shorts. Every time the guy that fell started moving toward the main beach, the blond guy would swoop over and crowd him away. Maybe the judges couldn't see it, on account of where they were sitting, but from the other side of the jetty it was clear as day that he was trying to force that poor fella into the cove."

Championship officials did not reply to our request for a comment.

For a minute, it feels like there's no air left in the room. It's the story we've all heard before: Shotgun hotdogging in the waters off the cove, losing his footing, and slamming into the jetty with enough force to shatter three bones in his left leg. He had memory loss afterward, due to the concussion, and only started spreading rumors about Flash when the championship lineup was announced and our uncle was placed in the top seed. It was a case of sour grapes, pure and simple . . . or so we've always been told.

The three of us just keep staring at one another. Finally, Xavier clears his throat. "'Blond hair and blue shorts' is a pretty vague description. It could be anybody—"

"It's Uncle Flash," Ruby cuts him off, swiping at the tablet a couple of times and then spinning it around again. On the screen, called forth from somewhere in the bowels of the internet, is a photograph: a group of surfers on Barton Beach, all smiles. The caption reads, "Entrants of the men's qualifying heats for the Regional Longboard Championship." Dead center, side by side, are Shotgun and Flash—fifteen years younger, but still recognizable—and our uncle wears royal-blue board shorts, his hair bleached into spikes so blond they're practically white. In fact, he's the *only* surfer who matches that description.

My stomach drops. "This doesn't . . . I mean, that doesn't

prove anything! Who's this witness, anyway? *That's* the guy who could be anybody. Why wouldn't he want anyone to know his name?"

"Maybe because surfing is a religion in this town, and your uncle was basically its archbishop back then," Xavier answers. When I glare at him, he holds up his hands in a mock surrender. "I'm just saying! Nobody likes talking about that day. My dad is the lifeguard they quoted—he's, like, literally a hero, and even *he* doesn't like to talk about it."

"It's true." Ruby swipes the picture off the screen. "It sounds like there were no other witnesses—or at least no one else willing to come forward. People loved Uncle Flash; he was a big hero. Nobody wants to think their hero could do something bad."

"You're not saying you believe this, are you?" I demand, shocked by her betrayal.

"You're kinda proving the point she's trying to make, dude." Xavier winces apologetically and then shuts up when I glare at him.

"Shotgun doesn't even remember what happened to him! He just read this and got ideas. He smeared Flash because he was a glory hound who was losing his shot at fame, while his biggest rival took home all the trophies." Even as I say it, though, I can remember the look on my uncle's face as he said, *Maybe I'll break your other leg tonight.*

It would finally explain why my dad has been so lenient with Shotgun over the years, letting him hog the bar at the Beachcomber and rarely making an issue out of the guy "forgetting his wallet" after running a tab. I'd always thought it was part of some townie code, or even his way of sticking it to Flash—letting his archrival get comfortable in the restaurant he was supposed to be helping out with. But maybe it was just Dad's way of apologizing for the past on behalf of the whole Fremont family.

But could my uncle really have been capable of something so underhanded?

"It doesn't really matter if he remembers or not, does it?" Xavier counters. "You keep telling us he did it, and the cops won't listen—well, here's why! Even if you don't think Flash was capable of running him into the jetty, Shotgun obviously believed it."

"Um . . . there might be even more to it than that." Ruby gives me her most serious look. "Did you see the date that article was published? The championship heats were fifteen years ago *this week*, Zac. I mean . . . it's literally the anniversary of Shotgun's accident."

"And Uncle Flash ends up dead in the cove, where it all went down," I conclude.

"Poetic." Xavier picks up another potato. "Messed up, but poetic."

"Yeah." Sitting back, I can't resist looking at the back door again, thinking about the fight I witnessed—about Shotgun's threats and the way my uncle taunted him. "Now we just have to figure out how to prove it."

# SIX

My uncle might have been a Barton Beach hero, but he didn't exactly live a life filled with ticker-tape parades, champagne toasts, or any other hero stuff. He more or less retired from professional surfing when I was still in grade school, and after that, he kind of coasted for a while. He did some local commercials, worked at a car dealership until he got bored with it, and then ended up back on the beach. He taught surfing lessons, took the occasional day-labor gig unloading cargo at the docks in Franklin Harbor, and sold junk to tourists.

It was the life of a true bohemian—no office, no rules, no boss to answer to—which was exactly how he wanted it, but all that freedom meant he was also perpetually strapped for cash. And that was in spite of what he earned as part owner of the perpetually strapped Beachcomber.

I say all this by way of explaining that he lived in a pretty run-down one-bedroom bungalow on the south side not far from the train tracks, which he shared with his girlfriend, Paige. With peeling paint, the screens torn and warping out of shape in the window frames, it does not look like the home of a guy who held a key to the city.

But it's my first destination later that morning, as soon as I can escape the Beachcomber, because if anyone can tell me more about my uncle, it's Paige Dufresne. Even if things weren't great between them lately—*she's not my biggest fan right now, either*, he had said the last time I saw him—she was probably the person who knew him best. Besides, Shotgun had been coming into the restaurant all week long, running his mouth, and spoiling for the fight he eventually got. She'd be the one to know if he'd also been hassling my uncle lately, or making threats.

It's weird being at Flash's place—looking at his HANG TEN welcome mat, the ancient fish board propped outside the door, cracked and weathered with age. I can even smell him here . . . that weird mix of sea salt, sunscreen, and patchouli that seemed to linger in the air wherever he went. It takes a minute to swallow down the lump in my throat before I can bring myself to knock.

There's no answer at first, but just when I think no one's home, I hear the dead bolt click. The door cracks open, still secured by its chain, and Paige peers out at me. Her eyes are red rimmed, her face blotchy and pale, and she sounds impatient as she says, "Yeah? What is it?"

"Uh . . ." Okay, in light of what was going on, I didn't exactly expect a *joyful* greeting, but . . . seriously? "I just wanted to come by and see how you were doing, I guess? After what happened to Uncle Flash, I thought . . ."

"I'm doing lousy," she states when I don't quite finish the statement. "What do you think? I had the cops here earlier, telling me Flash was dead on the beach, and then 'Have a nice day.' Do you have any idea what that's like?"

Even though I know it's wrong of me, that maybe her attitude is just the grief talking, I still bristle. "Sort of, yeah?"

She just looks at me, blankly, and then she squeezes her eyes shut. "Look, Zac, I'm sorry. I don't mean to . . . it's just, I've got no idea what I'm supposed to be doing here, you know?"

"I know." Just like that, I soften a bit. The truth is, I've never really warmed up to Paige; like all of Flash's girlfriends, she's pretty in that seen-it-all kind of way he liked, but she's not the sort of person who makes it easy to break the ice. In the five years they've been together, I doubt we've had even as many one-on-one conversations. "It's really . . . hard to believe. They came and told us at the Beachcomber, and I mean . . . we could still see the cops out on the jetty the whole time."

Paige looks down at the ground, sucking a sharp breath through her nostrils. "No offense, but if all you wanted to do was check on me, I've got—"

"I—actually, I had some questions that I was hoping you could answer for me," I blurt, trying to keep her from shutting the door again. "Can I come in?"

"This isn't a great time." She cranes her gaze around through the gap allowed by the chain, like she's trying to see if there's anyone hiding behind me. "And what questions? What are you talking about?"

"Well . . ." I take an uncomfortable breath. "It has to do with what the cops said . . . about how it might not have been an accident?" I wait, but Paige just stares at me, her expression blank, and I stammer on, "Y-you know, how he might have been fighting with someone on the jetty before it happened?"

"What are you talking about?" Her knuckles go white where her hand grips the inside of the doorframe. "The cops said that? When?"

"This morning," I answer, baffled, feeling like we're somehow not speaking the same language. "First they said it could have been an accident, and then they told us about that witness who saw a fight on the jetty. But they—"

"Wh-what witness? What are you . . . ?" She trails off, staring at me some more, and all I can do is stare back. And then she's shutting the door, disengaging the chain, and swinging it open again. "Just come in already. Hurry up!"

She slams the door shut again the second I'm in their stuffy little entryway, but she blocks me from moving in any farther. The walls are plastered with photos—of Flash, of Paige, of them together and with their friends—as well as yellowing magazine and newspaper articles boasting of my uncle's many notable surfing accomplishments. It calls that story from the *Gazette* back to my mind, and I squirm unhappily.

"What's all this about a witness?" She tucks a hank of dark hair behind her ear, shifting from foot to foot. "The cops didn't say anything like that to me—they just said he turned up on the beach."

She makes it sound like an accusation, and I lift up my brows. "They didn't?"

"No! I just told you—" She checks herself, taking a breath. "What did this witness see? Exactly, I mean." Haltingly, I repeat what I remember from the deputies' visit, and by the time I'm done, Paige has chewed most of the polish off her thumbnail. "That doesn't make sense. How do they know Flash was out there if this . . . witness couldn't even say how many people he saw? I mean, they're grasping at straws!"

"Well . . . they *don't* know it was Flash," I point out, having said as much a moment earlier. She tucks her hair behind her ears again, and an uneasy feeling stirs in my gut. Even for someone who just lost her boyfriend, Paige is acting really squirrelly, and I can't help wondering why. It also bothers me that the cops didn't tell her about the witness, because I can't think of many innocent reasons they'd be keeping her in the dark about that part of their investigation. "They just said they have to examine all the possibilities." Cautiously, remembering what Ruby said, I add, "They're probably going to do an autopsy, too. Just to confirm cause of death."

"An *autopsy*?" Whatever color was left in Paige's face drains out of it in an instant. "Is that necessary—cutting him open?" She drags her fingers through her hair. "Oh, this is just perfect. They can't do that without getting permission, though, can they? Because I don't want—I mean, Flash wouldn't want that. I mean, he didn't even want to be cremated, you know, because it creeped him out to think about his body getting burned up?"

"I think they can do whatever they want, if they suspect foul play." I watch her carefully, my uncle's words in the back of my mind. *Hell, if Paige calls, don't even tell her.* Why *was* he avoiding his girlfriend that night? And why doesn't she want them to do the autopsy, if it might help prove what really happened?

All of a sudden, I find myself convinced that Paige is hiding something—I'm just not sure what.

"Great. That's all I need. How *convenient* for them, that they can do all that and not care about anybody's wishes." She must finally notice my look, because her eyes narrow. "Listen, Zac, you're still a kid, but the day's gonna come when you stop thinking the cops are your best friends, okay? They get in your business once, they'll just keep finding reasons to get *back* in, until they have an excuse to mess with you."

I nod a little, trying not to look as suspicious as I feel— and trying not to get completely ahead of myself, either. Her edginess might be due to the grief thing, for one, but also, like, the whole reason I'm here in the first place is because the deputies tried to imply Dad had something to do with Flash's death and wouldn't listen to me when I gave them a better suspect. They've decided what happened, and don't want to be bothered with anything else; I'm the only one who seems to really care about finding the truth. Maybe Paige isn't wrong to want the cops out of her business right now.

"Do you know if Shotgun had been giving Uncle Flash trouble recently?" I ask instead. "Like, harassing him, or threatening him, or anything like that?"

"No more than usual." Paige rolls her eyes. "At least, I don't think. But Shotgun was a bad penny, always turning up sooner or later. I mean, talk about somebody who needs to get a life. Why are you asking?"

"He jumped Flash outside the restaurant last night." I tell her about the brawl behind the Beachcomber, and the threats Shotgun made before he left. "It was a bad scene. I told the cops about it, but it's like they didn't believe me— or they didn't want to."

"It's because this pesthole of a town hasn't produced a true surfing legend since Shotgun smashed up his leg and Flash retired." She pulls a soft pack of cigarettes out of her pocket and lights one up—and I can't help notice her hands are a little shaky. "If the two of them actually got along, they could've robbed a bank together and the cops would've said it was a misunderstanding." Exhaling a puff of smoke, the entryway turning even stuffier, she says, "So, Flash was at the restaurant last night?"

Something about the way she asks it—a little *too* casually to be truly offhand—sends up a red flag in my mind. I don't know why my uncle didn't want to be found, and there isn't much point in lying for him now, but . . . for some reason, it makes me reluctant to give her the details. "He just dropped by for a minute. I guess he'd been on the beach."

"What'd he say?" She focuses on her cigarette, smoking it like there might be a prize at the end.

"Nothing about going for a swim in the cove," I say, deliberately missing her point. He *was* hiding, I realize . . . but I'm still not sure who from, or why he'd chosen the Beachcomber of all places, on a night when the entire town showed up. But maybe Paige knows why; if I can only trick her into telling me. "It's funny, actually . . . he was almost never at the restaurant, but last night it seemed like everyone was looking for him there."

Her mouth twitches. "Who's everyone?"

"Well, Shotgun, for one. They missed each other by about thirty seconds." *Until they didn't.* "A couple of the Double Barrel guys were in for happy hour, and they asked about him. Even Vincent Webb—he came to see Dad, and he asked about Flash, too. Both of you, actually."

"Vincent Webb?" Her eyes snap up to mine, and she coughs out a little smoke. "What do you mean he was 'asking' about us? What for?"

I'm hit with a wave of déjà vu—Uncle Flash in the walk-in, giving me the same sort of look and asking the same sort of question. Only, at this point, I can't tell if she's paranoid or if *I* am. "It had to do with this hotel thing, and the city council. It sounded boring."

"It won't be, if he's involved in it." Paige laughs, a little hysterically, and it isn't a pretty sound. "Kid, lemme give you your second bit of grown-up advice for the day: You don't want Vincent Webb in your business any more than the cops." She stabs her cigarette out in an already-overflowing ashtray perched on a nearby shelf, its contents spilling across the painted wood. "Look, thanks for stopping by, but you'd better get going. I've only had two breakdowns so far today, which means I gotta squeeze my third in before I go to work in an hour."

She unlocks the door and all but pushes me onto the porch as I say, "If you remember anything Shotgun might've said—"

"I won't," she declares. Then, for the first time, something like regret flickers in her eyes. "Zac, I'm sorry about your uncle. I know he was like an idol to you, or whatever—but he wasn't always a nice guy, and the more you look for reasons people might've hated him, the more you're gonna find. So take my third bit of advice and just quit."

And with that, she slams the door in my face.

—————

I'm still mulling all of this over as I head back down the front walk, starting to realize that maybe the puzzle I was putting together was more complicated than I'd previously thought. Paige was not acting normal—not even for someone dealing with the unexpected death of their boyfriend—and I don't know what to make of it. I don't even have enough information yet to know if there *is* something to make of it.

Flash was avoiding her, and she seems more *annoyed* by his death than bereaved—but does that amount to anything significant? And why *didn't* the cops tell her Flash might've been murdered? As his girlfriend, and moreover his roommate, she was the first person I thought to ask about whether he was being threatened recently. If they didn't even bring it up with her . . . does that mean she's a suspect, too?

All of this is what's taking up my brainpower as I reach the sidewalk, which is why I walk straight into someone without even seeing them in front of me. "Oh, sorry, man, I—"

The words freeze in my mouth when I look up and realize I'm talking to none other than Vincent Webb. Flashing me that shark-toothed Realtor's smile of his, he says, "No worries, champ. You're Zac, right? Luke's boy?"

"Uh . . ." For a moment, it feels like I conjured him up just by speaking his name inside. "Yeah?"

"Listen, I heard about your uncle, and I'm real sorry for your loss. He was part of the soul of Barton Beach, and a lot of people around here loved him." His words are kind, but the forced smile betrays his insincerity. I'm reminded of the time I overheard one of our cooks describe him as "sleazy." "If it's any consolation, a guy like him? He lived on the waves, and I think they're the only way he'd have appreciated going out."

I nod, unable to speak, and not just because that's sort of a tasteless thing to say—*Your uncle was probably really happy he got smashed to death against all those rocks and debris*—but because this is the second time in two days our paths have crossed. And I'm not sure I believe in coincidences anymore. "Thanks."

"Hey, is Paige in?" he breezes on. "I wanted to give my condolences, but I've been having trouble reaching her."

"Yeah," I say automatically. "But she has to leave for work soon."

"I won't be long." He claps me on the shoulder. "Nice seeing you, Zac. Stay in school, okay? You're making your dad proud."

Having run out of hackneyed platitudes, he strides up the walk to my uncle's front door, leaving me to wonder why he couldn't just send a card.

Leaving me to wonder just how well he actually knew Flash Fremont, the supposedly beloved pillar of the community.

Leaving me to wonder just how much, exactly, I haven't been told yet about what's going on in Barton Beach.

# SEVEN

When I get to the Beachcomber, there's still a couple of hours left before my shift is supposed to start, and I can't resist standing at the front windows and looking out at the jetty. The beacon blinks, waves crashing against the break-water, sending up plumes of seawater and foam. My stomach curdles, thinking about Shotgun being hurled against the stone slab base—about my uncle possibly being hurled *off*. If Flash was hiding when I found him . . . did that mean he knew his life might be in danger?

The sky is gray, thick clouds rolling overhead, and although it's not supposed to rain again, it'll probably be another slow night, with all the college kids avoiding the beach, thanks to the cold. It was chilly enough when I arrived, but the temperatures will only drop further as the sun sets—and our space heaters can't exactly re-create the Margaritaville experience they'll all be looking for.

Movement catches my eye, and I realize the gloomy weather hasn't yet scared away everyone; out near the water's edge, I see a lone figure strolling along the surf, a beat-up metal detector in his hand. And, just like that, something connects in my brain, and I realize who I need to talk to next about Uncle Flash.

I'm grabbing my coat again, on my way back to the door, when my dad emerges suddenly from the bar area. "Oh, good, you're here. Listen, I need you to refill the salt and pepper shakers. Haley was supposed to take care of it, but I'm pretty sure she forgot."

"Uh." I finish shoving my arm through my coat sleeve, not sure how he didn't notice I'm not exactly *here* here yet. "I was just running out, but I'll do it when I get back, okay?"

Dad's brows come together in a scowl. "No, Zac, not 'okay.' This is your job, so take care of it now, like I asked."

"My shift doesn't start for two more hours," I point out, scowling right back. It's practically the first time he's spoken to me since we found out Flash died, and he wants to get on my case about salt and pepper? "Why can't I do it when I'm actually on the clock? I won't even be gone that long—"

"You're always on the clock—what part of that don't you understand?" he fires back, tossing a gesture around the dining room. "This restaurant is what keeps our lights on, and you need to pull your weight, the same as anybody else! If something needs doing, I expect you to do it, and without the attitude."

"I came in two hours early after spending the whole morning making tortilla chips with our busted fryer, and you're giving me crap about not pulling my weight?" I cannot believe him. "I literally have one single thing to do, and then I'll come right back—and I'll *still* be early. If I'd done it first, you wouldn't have known the difference, and you wouldn't be on my case about it!"

"Well, guess what, bud? You don't get to decide when work needs to be done!" Dad exclaims. "While you were making those chips, I was arguing with the distributor about a beer shipment they messed up. And while you were gone all afternoon, doing whatever you wanted, I was *still* on the phone with the distributor—because that's how the bills get paid!" He slaps the back of one hand against the palm of the other. "When you run a business, you don't get the luxury of pushing off your responsibilities until you're in the mood for it, okay? You need to get that through your head!"

*I don't run a business,* I want to scream at him . . . but there'd be no point. As far as he's concerned, I'm just another resource he can pour into the Beachcomber, and anything going on in my life—like the possible murder of my uncle, for instance—is irrelevant.

Wrenching off my coat, I throw it onto one of the tables and stalk toward the kitchen, my face so hot it feels like my eyeballs are about to start roasting. "*Fine.* I'll fill up the salt and pepper shakers, since apparently the restaurant will implode if it doesn't happen in the next thirty minutes! And then we'll be all ready for the nonexistent diners—because no one wants to go to the beach when it's fifty degrees out and *dead bodies* are washing up!"

I wait for his outburst—for him to yell at me again or at least maybe acknowledge Uncle Flash—but instead, he just sighs. "You know, I'm not asking for miracles here, Zac. Just salt and pepper." He turns to head back to his office. "One day, you and Ruby will be running this place . . . Is it too much to ask that you actually care about it a little?"

It's a sucker punch that hits me in two different places—my sense of family guilt and an even greater sense of future dread. Frankly, I'd have preferred the outburst.

A few minutes later, angrily unscrewing salt and pepper shakers at a table by the host stand, I'm so engrossed in mentally rehearsing all the things I should have said during my argument with Dad that I don't even notice Ruby until she's right over my shoulder. "I heard you two fighting."

I jump about a mile, and when my heart slows down again, I shoot her a peevish look. "We weren't fighting. *I* was being reasonable, and Dad was interviewing for a new job as a power-tripping prison guard."

"I think he's sad, Zac." Ruby adjusts her glasses, looking down at the floor.

"Well, he's got a weird way of showing it." There's a bitter taste in my mouth. "He hasn't brought up Flash *once* since the deputies were here, and now he wants to yell at me for not taking my 'job' seriously enough?"

"I think he just doesn't like to cry, so he gets angry instead." Her expression is solemn. "It's easier for him. It makes him feel ... I don't know. Less like everything is falling apart?"

"Yeah?" I pause what I'm doing and give her a suspicious look. "Did you learn all that from your podcast?"

She just shrugs and then sniffles. "I don't like it when you two fight."

"Me neither." I sigh, spreading my arms and pulling her into a hug. She more or less crawls into my lap, and I stifle a yelp when her bony behind digs into my thigh. "Are *you* doing okay?"

"I'm sad." She sniffles again and wipes her face. "Not angry sad, just ... the normal kind. I miss Uncle Flash."

"So do I." There's more I mean to say, but my chest is hot and my throat closes, so I leave it at that for a while. "I love you, Ruby Roo."

"I know. I love you, too."

Outside, waves roll up the shore and gulls ride the wind—and all I can do is wonder what's going on in Dad's head. What could have made him as angry at Flash as he was yesterday evening? And how could he be acting this way after his own brother just died? Ruby gets on my nerves sometimes, but if anything ever happened to her, I'd be a mess.

I guess if there's anything I miss even more than my uncle, it's a time when I never had to ask myself questions like these.

———

For all my complaining, the salt and pepper shakers only take about twenty minutes to fill, and because Dad stays in his office the whole time, not even coming out once to check on me, I'm shrugging back into my coat the second the last one is finished. I just hope I'm not too late to catch the guy I want to talk to.

The wind on the beach is pretty merciless, whipping across the Atlantic like it's got something to prove, turning the froth into a cold, sticky mist that clings to my skin. Apart from a couple of tenacious surfers, a lady tossing a Frisbee for her dog, and some desultory seabirds, the surf and sand are empty all the way up to the pier. The man with the metal detector is nowhere to be seen, and reluctantly, I turn the other way—facing the jetty.

Spearing out from the coast, a few dozen yards of time-blackened stone slabs jut haphazardly into the water, ending at the tublike beacon that flashes its warning at the far end. People walk out there sometimes, when the weather's good, taking pictures back along the coast. And at least a few of our local tragedies have been the predictable accounts of Spring Breakers who have too much liquid courage, daring each other to tag the beacon on nights when the waves are sending spray fifteen feet into the air above the walkway.

There are the usual caution signs posted, of course—NO SWIMMING, NO SURFING, NO FISHING—but that's about it. If there was any crime-scene tape, it's all gone now. And nothing remains on the sand of the cove itself to indicate that my uncle was lying there just this morning. Looking at it now—the curving inlet backed by steep, grassy dunes, water surging around exposed rocks along the shoreline—you'd never know it was so deadly.

Under my coat, my stomach shrinks to the size of a jelly bean, and I shiver. *What was it like?* I can't seem to stop thinking about it, the macabre question a lightning rod for my thoughts, calling them back to it again and again. Vincent Webb seems to think my uncle would have found it honorable, somehow, to die in the water; but just imagining it makes my blood run cold.

The year I turned twelve, I grew three inches, and Flash decided it was time to upgrade my board. He liked to joke about how I was finally getting my "man feet," and needed something with enough room to accommodate them. Of course, he then also gave me an exhaustive lesson on how my new height also meant a shifting center of gravity, and how I needed equipment I could count on as my frame continued to fill out.

Surfing was maybe the only thing my uncle took seriously—and even then, he was joking around more often than he wasn't.

At least, until he took me out for my first session with the new board and I got so carried away chasing the breakers that I drifted too far south. By the time I realized how close I was to the mouth of the cove, the current was so strong I couldn't paddle fast or hard enough to get clear of it. Around me, the water seemed to move like a single organism, pulling me farther south, the beacon at the end of the jetty thrusting closer.

Just as my state of panic was reaching full bloom, Flash swooped in, diving off his own board and grabbing me from mine. I plunged into the surf, sucking down a mouthful of filthy salt water, my ankle tether snapping so tight it nearly flipped me upside down. In the next few terrifying moments, my uncle disconnected the line, and I broke the surface—coughing and gasping for air—just in time to watch my brand-new board get sucked into Dead Man's Cove.

*What the hell were you thinking?* he'd demanded once he'd dragged me all the way back to safety on the shore. I was dazed and crying, and he was gripping me like he was afraid I might still get pulled out of his arms. *Zac, you could've been killed!*

*I just . . .* I couldn't finish. Overcome with fear and adrenaline, my whole body had been shaking. *I didn't . . . I didn't see—*

*You have got to be paying attention* all the time! he'd shouted. *This is not a game, do you understand? The ocean is a living thing, and the cove is a predator; if you get too close to it, it* will *take you down. You need to learn its boundaries, and respect them. Always.*

Thinking back on it—how nimble he was on his own board that day, how close he got without becoming caught in the same riptide that had me—makes me think again about that story in the *Gazette*. About how he purposefully drove Shotgun into the mouth of the cove, *a predator,* apparently for the sake of getting a leg up in a competition. It's hard to reconcile both images of the same man.

"Hey, dude, what're you doing out here?" The voice comes from over my shoulder, and I spin around to see the guy with the metal detector has managed to find me, instead of the other way around. "I dunno if you noticed, but this ain't beach weather."

Grinning widely, he offers a somewhat-grubby fist, and

we do a complicated handshake I learned from my uncle. "Hey, Ludlow. How's it going?"

"You know." He shrugs, the wind plastering his thread-bare clothes against his slender frame. The look on his face is full of nervous sympathy, like he's not sure what to say to me right now. "It's spring break, so I'm getting a few extra handouts. I'm getting by."

Back in the late eighties and early nineties, it was Ludlow who was the archbishop of Barton Beach's primary religion. He isn't quite as decorated a surfer as my uncle, but his name still comes up in the occasional "Best of All Time" lists, and some old footage of him made it into a documentary about the sport that recently won some prestigious film festival awards. By all accounts, he was handsome, charming, and full of promise.

But that was a few head injuries and a lot of drugs ago, and these days he more or less lives full-time on the beach. When the weather gets really bad, he usually looks for a bed at one of the shelters, but otherwise, he has a tent set up near the pier that he calls home. It's not technically legal, but the cops have always looked the other way for him.

"Hey, listen, man. I'm real sorry about Flash." Ludlow glances past the jetty and into the cove, his eyes full of sympathy. "He was one of the greats, you know? First time I saw him on the water, I thought, 'Well, damn, there go my records.'"

"Thanks. I appreciate it." A lump forms unexpectedly in my throat, and I swallow it down. "He would've appreciated it, too. He had a ton of respect for you." Ludlow nods somberly, and we share a moment of silence. But the whole reason I came out here in the first place was to find him, and I can't afford to lose any time. "It was you, wasn't it? The witness who saw people fighting out on the jetty last night?"

It should've occurred to me as soon as the deputies brought it up, but I was still too shocked by the news about Flash to make the connection. I was too busy questioning what a witness could have seen in that weather to wonder why anyone was out on the beach in the first place. But Ludlow rarely goes anywhere else, if he can help it, and even the worst rain is no match for his doggedness.

"Yeah, I guess it was." He looks out at the jetty again, waves slapping against the angled rocks, and his eyes lose a little focus as he thinks. "I was standing just about here, matter of fact . . . Sometimes the storms wash stuff onto the beach that you can sell—like, real valuable stuff, from shipwrecks or whatever—and there's people who come out first thing every day to see what's turned up." With a self-deprecating smile, Ludlow continues, "I ain't really a morning person, so I come when the waves pick up and just wait. So it was probably around midnight when all this went down."

Automatically, I glance back at the jetty again. The end

of it is pretty far off, but we're only standing a dozen yards or so from where it connects to the shore—from where my uncle would have to have been dragged out onto it—if that's really what happened. "What did you see, exactly? Like, how long were you standing here?"

He screws up his face. "Well, I was going up and down the beach, so I only stopped here for a minute or so. Didn't even realize there was anyone out there at first, till I looked at the beacon, because when the light flashed I saw, like, person shapes?"

"How many?"

"Jeez, I dunno." He gives a baffled shrug. "At least two, but they were right on top of each other, so it was hard to tell. I mean, they were either dancing or trying to choke each other out, you know? And it wasn't romantic-type weather, is all I'm saying." A gull swoops low, changes its mind, and turns back. "Honest, I wish I could be more help. I didn't even think the cops took me serious, the way they were asking me all those questions—like, '*What were you on?*' and all that."

My heart sinks a little. I'd been hoping the deputies were holding back, like they do in the movies—only saying enough to get us rattled, hoping we'd blurt something incriminating when they secretly had way more information than they were letting on. It's kinda disillusioning to realize they told us exactly what they knew.

Frustrated, I dig my hands deeper into my pockets, trying to think what Ruby would do in this situation. All those true-crime podcasts she listens to, all the weird trivia about how random real-life cases got cracked . . . I've got an actual eyewitness, and I have to be able to think of something else I can ask. "I don't suppose you could tell if one of them had a limp?"

Ludlow raises his eyebrows, letting out a whistle. "You think maybe Shotgun?"

I give a shrug that I hope looks noncommittal, not needing this to get back to the guy. Ludlow loves to gossip. "Just thinking out loud. He hated Uncle Flash, though, didn't he? And they got into it earlier in the night, behind the restaurant."

"They did?" He switches the metal detector to his other hand. "Dang. Flash was a pretty unpopular guy lately, I guess." It's kind of a rude comment, under the circumstances, but I'm suddenly curious to know what he means. *Did my uncle have more than one enemy in town?* Before I can ask, however, Ludlow is already continuing, "Now that you mention it, though, Shotgun has been sorta . . . fixating on old times recently."

"Yeah?" Again, I try to downplay my reaction. "You mean, like, fifteen-years-ago 'old times'? The qualifying heats?"

Ludlow's brow knits suspiciously. "You know about that?"

"It's on the internet, dude," I tell him condescendingly, like it wasn't my kid sister who found it for me. "Just because nobody around here wants to talk about it doesn't mean it doesn't get heard."

"Well. It ain't just that nobody talks about it." Ludlow looks down at his feet—in sandals, despite the icy spray from the ocean. "There was a lot going on that day. The water was really busy, and it was pretty chaotic. Not every-body saw what happened. And not everybody who saw what happened knew what they were seeing, if you get me." He doesn't meet my eye. "It just looked like Flash lost control of his board for a minute. Like he went off course and almost hit Shotgun but managed to recover in the nick of time."

"While Shotgun went into the water," I supply, hollow inside.

"Yeah." Ludlow's no happier than I am. "I mean, anyway, that's the way it looked to most people, so that's the story most people wanted to remember. But if you knew Flash, if you knew what kind of surfer he was, how good he was at commanding his board . . ."

That memory replays in my mind again—of getting caught in the undertow and Flash saving me, somehow coming right up against the currents himself without losing control. My stomach twists into a clove hitch, and I keep my back to the cove. "Got it. So Shotgun basically had a long history of good reasons to hate my uncle—is what you're saying?"

"Well, look, man." Ludlow sighs, obviously uncomfortable. "That was a weird time, and those two were always at each other's throats. Shotgun smashing up his leg was a big deal, but everybody seems to forget the time he dosed Flash to try to get him disqualified from the North Coast Surf Classic, or the time he almost ran your uncle off the road on the way back from a heat in Franklin Harbor."

It's the first time I'm hearing about either of these, and I goggle at him. "Are you serious?"

"Like I said, they were always at each other's throats. It wasn't a one-sided deal." He glances up the coast. "Anyway, once Flash retired, the rivalry died down a bit, but . . . yeah, if you're asking, it does seem like I've heard Shotgun grinding the old ax a lot more than usual lately."

"How often?" I ask, and then decide I might as well just get right to it. "Do you think he could've been the one out there on the jetty?"

"Could've? Sure," Ludlow says. "But it *could've* been anyone, pretty much. And, like I said, your uncle wasn't exactly the most popular dude on the beach last night."

It's the second time he's brought it up, and this time

I don't let the opportunity pass. "What are you talking about?"

"I just mean that, well . . . everybody knows how much he was fighting with your dad lately, for one thing." The way he says it, I can tell he thinks it won't come as a surprise, but a cold sweat prickles the base of my neck. How come *everybody knows this*? "But, also, Shotgun was apparently not the only dude who wanted a piece of Flash Fremont yesterday." Gesturing up the beach, he adds, "Last time I saw your uncle—like, up close and alive—was probably around eight p.m. or so, when he was trading punches with some college kid under the pier."

"What are you talking about?" I ask, a little stupidly, thinking about Flash's black eye. "He broke up a fight last night . . . Maybe that's what you saw."

"Uh . . . I know what breaking up a fight looks like, dude, trust me." Ludlow chuckles a bit, giving me a wry smile. "This was some foulmouthed Spring Breaker trying to knock your uncle's block off. Those rich boys don't know how to brawl, but all those glamour muscles can do some damage if they actually land a punch."

It feels like the beach is turned upside down, yet another fact I'd taken for granted about Uncle Flash cast into sudden doubt. Why did he lie to me about his black eye? Was he actually hiding from a *Spring Breaker* when I found him in the walk-in? It doesn't seem possible. Once again,

I've got so many questions I'm not even sure I know what they all are. "What'd the guy look like? And what were they fighting about? Do you know?"

"He was just a Spring Breaker." Ludlow seems confused by the question. "You know what they look like: short hair, sweatshirt with some kind of university logo on it, cargo shorts, sandals." He has just described 75 percent of the guys who we'll see at the Beachcomber this week. "As for what they were fighting about . . . man, I didn't get it. The kid was shouting at Flash, calling him a thief and all that—and then he said something about, like, seashells."

*"Seashells?"* I actually squint at him.

"I told you I didn't get it." Ludlow huffs a laugh. "I didn't hear him wrong, either, though. He shouted it a few times—*'something something seashells'*—while he was going after it with Flash."

"Seashells," I repeat it again, hoping it'll make more sense . . . but of course it doesn't. "Could the Spring Breaker be one of the guys you saw on the jetty?"

"Maybe." Another gust of wind sends the spray flying, and Ludlow finally reacts to it, hunching his shoulders. "But I'm telling you he didn't actually know how to fight, and unless he had some way better shoes somewhere, there's no way he could've kept his footing out there on the jetty in the middle of a storm. Not while tangling with Flash Fremont."

"Would you recognize the guy if you saw him again?"

I'm grasping at straws, and I already know what his answer will be before he starts shaking his head.

"It was dark, and I didn't get a close look. Sorry, bud." He thumps me on the shoulder. "Listen, I gotta get out of this wind for a bit. You hang in there, okay? And hit me up anytime you need a friend—I owe that much to Flash."

On that note, Ludlow says his goodbyes and starts back up the beach again, trailing his metal detector over the sand at the water's edge—leaving me behind with even less of a clue about what happened to my uncle than before.

# EIGHT

So far, all the evidence I've come up with to support my theory that Shotgun killed my uncle has been circumstantial. There's his history of aggressive and violent behavior toward Flash, for one, and the recent escalation of his grudge, for another. And then there's the fact that it turns out his grudge was probably sort of justified all along, and that he actually jumped my uncle right in front of me—*the very night he was later killed.* I mean, as far as I'm concerned, it all adds up.

But on the other hand . . . if some Spring Breaker tried to start something with Flash, I don't know why he would've made up a story instead of just telling me the truth—even if he lost the fight.

I don't know why he was avoiding Paige, why Paige got

so weird when I brought up Vincent Webb asking about the two of them, or why Webb seems to have had an interest in the two of them to begin with.

Maybe I'm just so desperate for answers that I'm finding them first and then coming up with questions to connect them to after.

And then there's my dad. As much as I hate to admit it, he *was* pretty obviously pissed at Flash—and he also pretty publicly said something that sounded like *We'd be better off if he was dead* only a few hours before he was killed. I don't believe for a second that Dad had anything to do with it . . . or, at least, that's what I'm telling myself. But I also don't know where he was at the actual time my uncle died. And if I'm being honest, I don't think I want to look for that answer yet, because I'm not sure I'll like what I find.

But again, if there's one person who seems to be central enough in all this that they might be able to tell me more, it's Paige Dufresne. And even though she kind of made a point to avoid telling me everything she knew the last time we talked, she's got no idea how annoying I can be when I want something. And I've recently started listening to some of Ruby's podcasts to hone my questioning skills.

---

Like I said before, there isn't much to Barton Beach west of the boardwalk, but there are the usual dive bars, strip malls, and fast-food joints that ugly up the main drag on the way to the interchange. That's where I head the next day, my bike frame rattling a bit because it desperately needs repairs I can't afford. Once again, my shift starts in a couple of hours—but this time I'm not making the mistake of stopping at the restaurant first.

The Tiki Touchdown is about a half mile in from the coast, and it's pretty much exactly what it sounds like: a tiki/sports bar. Mai tais are five bucks during happy hour, and a football game is reliably playing on one of the seven wide-screen TVs no matter what time of year it is. Paige has been a waitress there since pretty much the time she met Flash, and even though she hates it, she's never tried to get a job anywhere else.

They're closed when I arrive, but the guy at the door is another townie—someone who knew Flash well enough to recognize me as his nephew—and he guesses why I've come. "Looking for Paige? She's taking a smoke break out back. *Another* smoke break."

He says it like it should mean something to me, like we're supposed to disapprove together or something. So I roll my eyes and shake my head—*that Paige*—and then circle around to the narrow alley that runs along back. All the businesses on this stretch share this alley, where everything reeks of trash, motor oil, and patrons who didn't feel like standing in line for a urinal.

Paige is sitting on a dented barstool when I find her

at the back door of the Touchdown, a cigarette dangling from her lips as she furiously works at a scratch ticket she's spread across her knee. When she catches sight of me, her brows shoot up . . . and then immediately knit together. "What the hell are you doing here?"

"Nice to see you, too." Her attitude is making me cranky. I don't have to be patient with her grief, I've decided. Not when I've got my own to deal with. "What'd Vincent Webb want to talk to you about yesterday?"

The coin she's using on the scratch ticket slips, and she glances up again. It's weird, like an instant replay of Flash looking at me in the freezer through a bag of frozen peas. "None of your business."

"That's funny. He told me he was dropping by to pay his respects." It's bait, and she knows it, her mouth tightening until her lips lose their color. She finishes the scratch ticket, frowns at it, and then throws it into a trash can next to the stool. Immediately, she pulls out another scratch ticket from her apron and starts in on that one. "Did he bring up the hotel thing?"

It's the only other key word I can think of that Flash might have been reacting to, and it definitely presses one of Paige's buttons as well. Sitting up, her eyes flicker. "What do you know about 'the hotel thing'? What did Flash say to you that night?"

I fight the urge to raise my brows. According to Ruby,

sometimes detectives break a case just by throwing random stuff out and seeing how people react—the problem is, I don't exactly know how I'm supposed to bluff Paige into revealing more when I've already played all the cards I've got in my hand. "He didn't tell me much, but I know he was avoiding Webb. And you."

"And what the hell is that supposed to mean?" Paige throws the new scratch ticket away as well, glaring at me. "What are you trying to say, Zac? Just come out with it."

"He said if you asked where he was, I shouldn't tell you." I cross my arms over my chest, suddenly feeling small when I think I'm supposed to be at my most intimidating. "Why would he say that?"

Paige closes her eyes and rubs her brow, taking a drag on the cigarette before stubbing it out under her shoe. Curtly, she says, "We got in a fight, okay? He did something stupid, and I told him what I thought about it, and then I told him to get out. And then he never came home, and I thought he was teaching me a lesson, until the cops showed up." When she looks at me again, her eyes are a little wet. "There. Happy now?"

Digging my toe into the edge of some old gum that seems all but fused to the pavement of the alley, I ask, "What'd he do?"

Paige doesn't answer right away. She lights another cigarette and then pulls yet another scratch ticket out of her apron, grinding away at it with the edge of her quarter. "It doesn't matter. Just forget about it."

"If it doesn't matter, why was he hiding at the Beach-comber?"

"Give it a rest, okay?" Paige tosses her hands in the air. "The point is that he never learned how to control his impulses, because somehow, things always broke in his favor. Until they didn't." The latest ticket is apparently also a bust, and she throws it into the trash with the others. "Why are you asking all this stuff, Zac? What do you think you're going to figure out—that your uncle could be an idiot sometimes? Well, congratulations, you've cracked that case wide open."

"The cops think Dad had something to do with what happened to him," I finally admit, my voice embarrassingly thin. "Or at least that's the way they made it sound. I told them I thought it was Shotgun, and they ignored me."

Paige snorts, and yet another ticket emerges from her apron. "I told you before that plenty of people had it in for Flash."

"My dad didn't *have it in* for him—"

"Yeah, he did." She rolls her eyes at me. "You don't want to see it, because you're fourteen and—"

"I'm *six*teen."

"—you still think the world is like a clock, where everything runs on time, and if there's a problem, you fix it."

Dragging on the cigarette, blinking against the smoke, she continues, "But it's a mess, okay? Everything's a mess, and nothing's messier than family. Your dad was pissed at Flash because what Flash did best was messing up and counting on the rest of us to forgive him for it. And sometimes he pushed people too far."

Startled by the cold vehemence in her tone, I take a step back. "What are you saying?"

"Stop thinking that 'reliable old Luke Fremont' wouldn't hurt a fly, because he absolutely would, just for starters. He could be a real SOB—and if you don't believe me, you should ask *him* about 'the hotel thing.'" The last of the scratch ticket's windows is revealed, and Paige curses at it, hurling it into the trash with its counterparts. "Secondly, I'm saying that what you're doing is pointless, and kind of sad. You think you're some sort of detective? You're gonna find out what happened to Flash? Lemme help you again: *Flash* happened to Flash." She gets up, stubbing out her new cigarette, even though it's only half-smoked. "He was selfish and self-involved, and he never thought about the consequences of his actions—not the ones that hurt him, and *definitely* not the ones that hurt anybody else. Just be glad you're not the one he—"

She catches herself, snapping her mouth shut abruptly. And then she starts for the back door of the Touchdown, and I scramble after her. They won't let me into the bar, and she knows it. "Wait!"

"Don't waste any more of your time, Zac." Looking back at me, she grits her teeth. "I mean it. This town chews people up, even the ones it loves. You've still got a whole life to live . . . don't waste it on Flash Fremont, and don't waste it on Barton Beach."

The door slams shut behind her, and once again, I'm alone—and I don't feel like I had any of my questions answered. Or, at least, I didn't get any of the answers I wanted, and what I did get is making my stomach hurt. *Stop thinking that "reliable old Luke Fremont" wouldn't hurt a fly, because he absolutely would.*

It's not like I don't notice that, by bringing all that up and throwing my dad under the bus, she avoided answering any of my other questions. I still don't know what Webb came to see her about, I still don't know why Paige was mad at my uncle, and I don't know any more about "the hotel thing" than I did when Dad explained it to me the other night.

*You should ask him about "the hotel thing,"* she had said. What scares me is that I'm starting to think she's right. There has to be more to the situation than just what I've been told so far or people wouldn't keep reacting this way when I bring it up.

But what if I learn something I really don't want to?

I'm turning to go, ready to grab my bike and head back to the beach for another night of trying not to stare out the window at the beacon on the jetty, when something in the trash can catches my eye. I don't know exactly what it is that compels me to take a closer look—Ruby would call it intuition, and her podcasts are full of accounts where a little unexplained curiosity led to a case's Big Break—but I lean over and peer inside.

There's something written on the back of one of Paige's discarded scratch tickets.

54234-675898-222-6

**WINNER'S INFORMATION**
Please print information clearly

In order to claim cash prize for a winning ticket, submit the ticket to its original place of purchase or to your local Lottery Commission office. Winning tickets can also be submitted via mail to any state Lottery Commission office. Claimant must provide proof of ID and be at least eighteen years old on date of purchase. See state Lottery Commission website for full terms and conditions.

PRINTED NAME: _____

ADDRESS: _Bel Mondo International_
_____ _$80K???_

PHONE NUMBER: _____

SIGNATURE: _____

# NINE

I'll admit that, at first, I don't know what to make of the note. Well, at first, I don't make *anything* of it. Scrawled on the back of a scratch-off ticket in Paige's spidery handwriting, it just looks like a gambling tip. Bel Mondo International could be anything from a racetrack to a film studio—and whatever my uncle did or didn't do, he never once had eighty thousand dollars in his hands. I file it away, deciding to look up the name later.

Besides, even if Dad would never notice the difference between me showing up two hours early and me showing up thirty minutes early, he will absolutely notice me showing up thirty seconds *late*. And I have one more stop to make before I head to the restaurant.

The beach and boardwalk are what keep this town

on the map, and what make people want to stay here, despite the lack of real opportunities, but during the high season, you couldn't pay the locals to go anywhere near the sand. Nobody wants to finish an eight-hour shift at the brewery or the recycling plant and then go drink a beer while surrounded by shrieking, inebriated tourists who are experimenting with no inhibitions.

Like all the good townies, Uncle Flash had a regular hangout that was nowhere any self-respecting Spring Breaker would dare to tread—either on purpose or by accident. Located on the south side, sandwiched between a pawnshop and a laundromat that's been closed for so long it might as well be condemned, the Double Barrel Saloon is an institution.

Chaining my bike up out front, knowing I might return to find it stripped of its tires, I shoulder my way through the door. Despite the fact that there's no bouncer to check my ID, I'm taking it a little bit on faith that I won't get thrown out, but as Flash Fremont's nephew, I have a feeling the guys inside will be glad to look the other way.

I find them bellied up to the bar—all of my uncle's best friends, ranging in age from thirtysomething to sixtysomething: Carlos, Ziegler, Spitfire, and Gravy. A half-empty bottle of rotgut whiskey sits open in front of them, and they're in the process of pouring out a round of shots when I join them.

"Hey, Sparks!" Ziegler greets me with the nickname that never quite took. They gave it to me when I was nine, crashing around in the surf on my boogie board, swearing I was going to be as good as my uncle someday. Flash and Sparks . . . but these guys are the only ones who ever used it. "It's good to see you, dude. Sit down."

"Yo, Freddie," Gravy calls to the bartender. "We need another glass over here for Sparks!"

"Don't bust my chops, man." The bartender gives us an aggrieved look. "He shouldn't even be in here, and you know it. I don't need to lose my license again." To me alone, he adds, "You touch a drop, you're out. Got it? I'm not playing around."

I cross my heart. "I got it."

"C'mon, man, it's a wake!" Carlos complains anyway. "We're drinking to the memory of a legend over here. The kid's uncle just died, for Pete's sake."

"Next guy who hassles me is out, too." Freddie points at him.

"I'm not staying," I promise. "I just wanted to drop in and see the guys for a minute."

"Hey, man, to your uncle." Spitfire raises his glass, his eyes already looking a little soft-focus. "It's a hell of a thing. He was the greatest surfer this town ever saw. The greatest it ever turned out, anyway."

The glasses go up, and they drink, and Freddie pours

me a soda—free of charge—so I can join them. There are things I want to know and not a lot of time left for me to ask questions, but as the round is refilled, they start sharing stories about Flash . . . and for a while, I just listen. Spitfire brings up the time my uncle got drunk and streaked the boardwalk; Carlos brings up the year he got engaged three times to the same woman; Ziegler lists off all the records he set on the water.

"He's the reason I'm still alive." Gravy is drunk, but his tone is sober. "That time I fell off my board and blacked out in Waikiki, Flash is the one who dragged me out of the water and did mouth-to-mouth until I came to again." He raises his glass one more time. "Only time a guy ever kissed me, and it was worth it!"

It's a story I've heard before, but it takes on a new meaning now that my uncle isn't around to brag or downplay it, or make a joke about Gravy's bad breath. All the stories mean something different now—and my eyes mist over as I realize that, for the first time in a few days, I'm surrounded by people who actually seem to miss him.

"Does anybody know what he was doing on the beach that night?" I finally ask, once they're all good and tipsy and there's a lull in the conversation. "I saw him at the Beachcomber around nine o'clock, and apparently he never went home after that."

They all exchange a blank look, and Ziegler shrugs. "No

idea, man. He spent as much time as he could on the water, though. Maybe he just wanted to wait till all the Spring Breakers were gone so he could have it to himself."

It hits me that none of them know about the struggle on the jetty, because so far the cops haven't made it public knowledge. I debate bringing it up, but then I decide not to; I don't want to influence the way they hear my next question. "Was Shotgun giving Flash any extra trouble recently? I heard he wasn't handling the anniversary of his injury all that great."

Again, the guys exchange a look—wary, this time—and Carlos mutters, "Not that I heard. But, you know, that story is complicated, and the two of them . . ."

He trails off, and nobody picks up the thread, so I try again. "The two of them . . . what? Look, Shotgun was coming into the restaurant a lot lately, looking for trouble—more than usual. I know they had history, but it seems like things were a lot worse between them lately, yeah?"

Suddenly, they're all really interested in their empty glasses, not one of them looking my way, and I begin to lose my patience.

"Listen, I know there's, like, a Surfer Code, or whatever, but I watched Shotgun tackle my uncle to the ground and pound his head into the beach that night!" I exclaim. "And then a few hours later, Flash turns up dead in the cove—where he was way too smart to get caught—and nobody wants to admit how suspicious that looks? I'm sick of people pretending like it didn't mean anything that Shotgun was always running his mouth about my uncle and saying he wanted to kick his—"

"Nobody's saying it didn't mean anything," Carlos interrupts me, putting his hands up. "You want my opinion? Shotgun hated Flash for sure, but not enough to do . . . you know, what I think you're suggesting. He just spent so much time nursing that grudge that he didn't know how to live any other way."

"With Flash gone, Shotgun's not gonna know what to do with himself," Gravy chimes in. "You won't believe this, dude, but he once decked a guy for saying Flash didn't earn his title in the Stokely Invitational—and that was five years *after* his leg got busted up."

Ziegler nods. "Like the man said: Things were complicated."

I sit back, speechless, staring at the streaked mirror behind the bar. This is the first time I've ever heard anything about Shotgun *defending* Flash—at any time, for any reason—and I don't know what to make of it. That scene behind the Beachcomber keeps coming back to me, the blood and the threats and the fury crackling in their eyes. It feels too urgent to ignore just because people want to think of their mutual antagonism as a stable equation.

Either way, these guys are not going to help me build

a case against Shotgun—at least, not intentionally. But that doesn't mean they don't know something that can help me anyway. "Well, was he getting hassled by anyone else? Ludlow told me he saw some Spring Breaker tangling with Flash under the pier that night."

"Well." Carlos makes a face. "Ludlow."

"'Well, Ludlow,' what?" I make a face of my own.

"You can't necessarily take what that guy tells you at face value, is all." He squirms a little. "I mean, I like the guy, but . . . his brain is fried, man. Drugs messed him up pretty bad."

"They gotta clean the beach up," Ziegler adds, scowling. "He could've been competing a lot longer if he'd managed to kick the habit."

"So you think he was lying?" I stare at them.

"Not lying, just . . . sometimes he's not the most reliable witness, is all," Gravy puts in.

For a moment, I'm stunned into silence. Is it possible Ludlow imagined everything? *They were asking me all those questions—like "What were you on?" and all that.* For the first time, I consider that maybe the reason the cops didn't mention the altercation on the jetty to Paige is because it just . . . didn't happen. I still can't believe Flash would have gone out on the water voluntarily during a storm, but what if I have all the facts wrong to begin with? What if I've put all my eggs in a basket with a hole in it?

My heart sinks, and I stare at my barely touched soda, a dull ache forming in my chest. Maybe I only believed Ludlow because I want so badly for there to be a *reason* that my uncle died. I want it to make sense somehow, when maybe it just never will.

"I mean"—Spitfire makes a listless gesture—"even if Ludlow was right, there's no accounting for what Spring Breakers will get up to when they have enough beer in 'em."

The rest of the guys mumble an agreement, and Gravy gives me a sympathetic look. "Truth is, Sparks, if someone was really gunning for your uncle recently, we wouldn't know about it. Flash hadn't been around here for a while—and just lately, anyway, he'd been dodging my calls."

"Mine, too," Carlos says, and then Ziegler and Spitfire cosign this as well.

Once again, I'm speechless. It's not like I kept tabs on my uncle's whereabouts, but he'd been hanging out right here at this same bar a few nights a week for as long as I can remember—literally. "He'd stopped coming to the Double Barrel? Why?"

"I dunno." Ziegler shakes his head. "He just . . . didn't show one day. And then he didn't show the next, and . . . you know, so on."

"Well, when's the last time you saw him?"

"It was probably that cargo job in Franklin Harbor," Spitfire suggests, and the other guys murmur an agreement. "Foreman at the docks needed a few extra guys to help unload a ship with a tight turnaround, so he got in touch and the five of us went down."

One of the many ways my uncle managed to stay afloat was taking day-labor gigs when the need arose and the offers came in. Painting houses, landscaping, moving furniture for college kids in Franklin Harbor . . . contrary to what my dad always claims, Flash didn't actually hate to do real work—he just hated real obligations.

"Would've been two weeks ago, Sunday." Gravy does the calculations. "Got me out of driving my mom to church."

"You'd've been struck by lightning before you made it through the door," Spitfire quips with a snort. "Vincent Webb did you a favor."

"Webb?" My ears perk up. Why do I keep coming across his name?

"Yeah, it was his ship." Spitfire refills his glass. "Or, at least, it was his cargo we were busting our butts to unload."

"Guy owns a restaurant, some motels, and a handful of souvenir stands, but we might've been carrying cannonballs for how heavy that crap was." Carlos pushes his glass in front of Spitfire as well.

"Was Vincent Webb there?" I ask next, still trying to figure out how he connects to my uncle. Or, rather, why he *keeps* connecting with my uncle. The man has a sleazy air, and there are plenty of rumors that his business dealings aren't always "clean," but half of Barton Beach is either owned, employed, or funded by Webb in some capacity. It's not exactly a shock that it was his cargo—or even that he might offer his condolences on Flash's passing.

But if once is chance and twice is a coincidence, then three times in as many days makes his involvement a pattern.

"Nah, man." Ziegler chuckles at my question. "Guys like him don't spend time at the docks—nobody does, if they can help it. Hell, Flash didn't even stick around that day."

"What do you mean?"

"He took his cut early and split." Carlos swipes his hand through the air. "Said he pulled a muscle or something—like, tweaked his back? Anyway, he was in too much pain to finish the job. It sucked, too, because he was the one that drove us all down, and we had to cadge a ride home."

None of it adds up. I've already checked my own memory bank for two weeks ago, Sunday, and I remember seeing Flash on the beach that very evening. Zipped into his wet suit, with his board under his arm, he was in high spirits—ready to catch as many sunset waves as he could before losing the beach to the Spring Breakers for the rest of the season. Bumping his fist against mine, he'd grinned ear to ear, telling me, *This is the year we all get rich, bud—I can feel it in my bones!*

But why would he make up a back injury to his friends

to get out of a job he had no real responsibility to do in the first place? He could've just said he didn't feel like working that day, and not one of these guys would've held it against him. So if we're talking chances, coincidences, and patterns, well . . . this is now the second time I've learned that he chose to tell a lie when there was no actual reason to. I mean, sure, maybe he needed to sell his excuse to the foreman, but it's exactly the kind of harmless dishonesty he'd have owned up to afterward . . .

If he hadn't also inexplicably stopped hanging out with his friends at the same time.

"So nobody saw him again after that Sunday?" My mood deflates a bit as I start to worry that I'm running out of places to look. I still have nothing solid against Shotgun, and everywhere I turn, I come away with a dozen new questions for every one answer I get. I'm sure Paige is keeping something from me, but I don't have any leverage on her, and my number-two suspect is an anonymous—and possibly fictitious—Spring Breaker with an anger problem.

Or Dad. But I can't go there.

But then it's Freddie, the bartender, who surprises me. "Actually, I did see him. About five days ago, maybe—not here, but down at the beach. He was selling seashells to some of the tourists over by the pier."

"Huh?" I blink at him, wishing I could have come up with a more elegant way to phrase the question.

"Yeah. He was carrying them around, showing them off . . . seemed to be making pretty good money, too." Freddie grins in devilish respect. "I must've seen at least four girls pay him for something they could've just dug up out of the surf on their own. Talk about a racket—that guy could've sold pearls to an oyster."

"Like I said," Spitfire rejoins, "there's no accounting for what Spring Breakers will do when they have enough beer in 'em!"

Gravy chuckles into his whiskey. "Man, that Flash was something else. Always had some kind of a side hustle going—you gotta respect the game."

"Some kind of side *racket* is more like it." Ziegler laughs and lifts his glass again. "To Flash, Barton Beach's greatest surfer and biggest operator! May he rest in peace."

"Hear, hear!" The rest of the guys toast my uncle's memory, downing the whiskey in lusty gurgles—and then they're on to the next memory, the next off-color story about Flash's off-color exploits.

And I just stare at my streaky reflection in the mirror behind the bar—thinking maybe Ludlow *was* on the money after all, about both the fight on the jetty and the Spring Breaker under the pier. But I'm also forced to wonder why anyone would attack my uncle over a seashell in the first place. Why Flash would lie to me, cut off his friends, fight with Dad, and avoid his girlfriend? Why he would taunt

Shotgun after breaking his leg and ruining his career fifteen years ago, knowing how much it messed the guy up?

There's only one thing I'm certain of after coming to the Double Barrel today: I didn't know my uncle as well as I thought.

# TEN

By the time I make it back to the beach, gloomy and disheartened, I'm starting to wonder if maybe *Paige* was the one who was right all along: Maybe I should never have started looking into this. Nothing I've found will convince the cops that they should take Shotgun seriously as a suspect—that they should consider *anyone* other than my dad—and all of it has made me unhappy.

There's still an hour to go before my shift starts, and for a while, I just stand there on the beach, watching the restaurant—unable to go in early. Not again. Among the many depressing things I've heard over the past few days, the voice that echoes loudest in my ears is Dad's: *One day, you and Ruby will be running this place.*

When I was a kid, the Beachcomber struck me as just

the coolest thing in the world. I couldn't believe it *belonged* to us—that I could spend all day playing in the sand and then run inside for free soda and free snacks. While most people had to stay in the dining room and bar, I could go anywhere I wanted, even the employees-only parts that were forbidden to everyone else. Popular with the locals in the off-season, even my friends at school knew about the restaurant, its big, weather-beaten sign unmistakable from anywhere along the Barton Beach coastline.

I thought we were famous.

But lately, now that I'm older, it's stopped feeling like a secret hideout and started feeling like . . . well, kind of a trap. I see just how much of Dad's energy it eats up, how much of his time and our money. The busted fryer, the broken awning, the rickety pot rack in the kitchen . . . the lazy distributor, the roofing repairs, the slow nights. There's no more magic in being "the family that owns the Beachcomber." Most days—when I have to go in early to do prep, and then early again to refill napkin dispensers and clean tables, before working a full shift for no pay and a handful of measly tips—it feels like the Beachcomber owns *us*.

Is that really the future that I want? And even if I get to the bottom of my uncle's death, I'll still see the place it happened every time I come into work. When I think about what a life in Barton Beach did to Flash and Shotgun, to Paige and Ludlow . . . is that what's in store for me when all the debts and obligations that run Dad's life end up in my hands?

———

At least one of the conclusions I came to earlier in the day proves to be incorrect: The guys at the Double Barrel are not the only other people left in town who miss Flash Fremont. To kill some time, I follow yet another macabre impulse and wander back out to the south end of the beach again, where the jetty finally appears somewhat peaceful in the late-afternoon sun. At first, I think I'm just going to have another sad little emo moment, looking at the spot my uncle washed up and wishing I could do our final conversation over again, but instead, what I find startles me.

The shoreline of Dead Man's Cove consists mainly of rocks and shell fragments driven right up into the side of the dunes, leaving only a narrow crescent of flat beach that curves off the south side of the jetty. And there, tucked against the raised walkway, a makeshift shrine to Flash has flourished practically overnight. Candles and flowers, cards and photos . . . a massive collection of tributes have been piled together under a driftwood cross pounded into the sand. It's hard to know what my uncle would have made of it—a guy who wasn't particularly religious but loved attention in all its forms—but something twinges in my chest at the sight of it.

And then I go stiff when I recognize someone stooped

over the offerings, pawing through all the trinkets left to honor my uncle, tossing some aside and gathering others into his greedy hands. As if conjured by my dark thoughts, it's Shotgun McInnes.

Rage slaps against me like a tidal wave, taking out my common sense and propelling me forward, the whole world gone red. *"What the hell do you think you're doing?"*

Shotgun looks up just as I lunge at him, slamming my hands into his chest, shoving him as hard as I can. His feet skid a couple inches on the wet sand, but he otherwise barely moves, his body sturdier than one of the pilings holding up the pier. I come at him again, and this time, he drops the things he's holding so he can defend himself. "You lost your mind, kid? Get offa me!"

He knocks me back, and I almost go sprawling, my heart thundering in my ears. His upper body strength is unreal, and the shock of it is just enough to snap me out of my haze of anger. I'm lucky he didn't take a swing at me, or I could be picking up my teeth right now.

Still furious, but keeping my distance, I snarl, "Just get out—you don't belong here!"

"It's a free country." His nose is swollen badly, the bruises that cover it so dark they're nearly black in places, and he bares his teeth. "Anyway, I'm done letting Fremont trash tell me what to do. My crap luck is finally turning around for the first time in my life, and I don't give a damn what you want. You can go to hell along with your uncle."

Shaking from fury, I ball my hand into a fist, not sure how I could ever have felt sorry for this guy. "You're a loser, you know that? You've wasted your whole life throwing a nonstop pity party for yourself and trying to get back at Flash—because you've got nothing else, do you?"

"Screw you, you little punk!" Shotgun stomps forward—and I'm not proud of it, but I flinch. "Your uncle was a liar and a scumbag, and all this stuff"—he waves a gesture at the shrine—"is a damn *joke*. All Flash ever cared about was himself: not this town, not these people, and not even you. So call me a loser all you want, say I wasted my life . . . at least I didn't waste it trying to butt-kiss a sleazy, under-handed cheat—"

*"Shut up!"* I roar in his face, furious tears pricking my eyes, pushed right back beyond my ability to reason, just like that. "It was you, wasn't it? You told him you'd finish what you started, and that's exactly what you did! You're the reason my uncle is—"

*"You watch your mouth."* Taking two huge steps forward, Shotgun twists my shirtfront up in one massive fist and pins me to the sidewall of the elevated jetty. "I had nothing to do with his death, you got it?" His eyes bulge, and he looks past me, toward the beacon. "I already told the cops: I

had too much to drink at the Beachcomber, and after Flash and I threw down, I went home to sleep it off. And that's where I was until the next morning when I heard the news, and that's that. You understand?" When I don't answer, he leans in closer, until we're almost nose to broken nose. "I said, *that's that.*"

My heart in my throat, the sharp stones of the jetty digging into my back, all I can do is struggle in vain to pry his hand away from my collar. "Let me go!"

"You wanna be mad at someone over what happened to Flash? Be mad at *him*," Shotgun growls in my face, "because he brought it on himself."

With that, he tosses me aside, kicks a path through the clutter around the shrine, and storms up the beach for the steps leading to the boardwalk. When he reaches the top, he casts one last look over his shoulder, and then disappears from view.

———

I stay down there for a while, reorganizing the memorabilia tucked around the base of the cross with trembling hands, not even sure what I'm doing other than distracting myself. It still angers me to think about Shotgun pilfering my uncle's tributes, even though none of it is worth much, and I can't imagine what he'd even want with it. Some of the stuff is brand-new—surfing-themed toys and key chains—and

I struggle to figure out what kind of person would spend money to leave junk on the beach. And the whole time, I kick myself over what I just did.

It was really stupid of me to confront Shotgun, and even stupider—possibly, anyway—to basically accuse him outright of killing my uncle. If he didn't know to cover his tracks before, he sure does now.

*I had nothing to do with his death . . . I already told the cops.* Maybe I ought to be encouraged by that, since it sounds like the deputies at least took my account seriously enough to talk to the guy, but "sleeping it off" isn't much of an alibi. Belatedly, it occurs to me that Shotgun is one of the only people I've encountered so far who isn't still assuming Flash's death was an accident. Does that mean the cops told him what Ludlow saw when they didn't even tell Paige?

Or does that mean he just gave himself away?

When I'm done with the shrine, I pull myself back up to the elevated path leading out to the jetty and glare in the direction that Shotgun went. From where I stand, about three feet higher than the beach itself, the roofs of some of the boardwalk businesses are just visible beyond the railing at the top of the staircase. There's a souvenir stand, a stall full of knockoff sunglasses, the saltwater taffy place . . . and then an electronics store, advertising calling cards and prepaid cell phones. It probably carries the most valuable merchandise along the entire strip, and to demonstrate its awareness of this, it's also the only establishment with external security cameras.

My eyes going wide, I realize that one of them is aimed at the jetty.

With forty-five minutes left to go until my shift starts— at which time, I'd better be *in* the Beachcomber, or my dad will begin offering my organs on the black market— I'm mounting the boardwalk, trying not to put too much thought into what I'm about to attempt. If you *think* you're guilty, you *act* guilty . . . or so Flash once told me a few years back, when he was helping himself to "free" samples at the saltwater taffy place.

The electronics store is best described as "intimate." Well, it's honestly best described as "cramped," the cabana-size interior crowded with displays of burner phones, portable chargers, replacement cables, and more. But space on the boardwalk is at an absolute premium, so they're not alone. And although I don't really have a clue what I'm doing as I push my way inside, there's one thing I'm sure I can count on: Anyone who's working here will be a townie, which means there's a 95 percent chance I already know them.

And, of course, I'm right.

"Zac?" Aditi Patel arches her brow from behind the counter. She's a year ahead of me at school, but we take band together, so we're not strangers. "Hey, dude. Uh . . . I'm sorry about your uncle."

"Thanks." I look around at the close walls, the shiny plastic of the hanging merchandise, the rectangular screen mounted in a corner just beneath the ceiling—a grainy security display of the room, and me looking back. "I didn't know you worked here."

"Yeah, well." Aditi shrugs with the resignation of every townie kid in a customer service job. "I applied at Starbucks first, but . . . so did everybody else. So now I'm selling prepaid phones to junkies on the beach. Another day in paradise, right?"

"Tell me about it." I'm hardly paying attention, my gaze fixed on that TV screen. "Um. Were you working here . . . you know, the other night? When my uncle . . . ?"

I don't have to finish. From the way she winces, it's clear Aditi understands what I mean. "Uh, no, dude. Sorry. I mean, I worked that afternoon, but the shop closes at eleven, so there probably wouldn't have been anyone here when your uncle . . . uh." She swallows. "I mean, if that's what you're asking."

"Yeah," I confirm awkwardly. Even though the cops are sitting on Ludlow's account for the time being, they're still using his estimate of "around midnight" as an unofficial time of death for Flash. But I really only asked that question as a segue to my next one. "Do those security cameras run all night long?"

"Uh." Aditi's eyes go wide. "Yeah? I think so? Dude . . . you're not—"

"One of them is aimed at the jetty." I'm sure my face is bright red, and I can't quite look her in the eye.

"Yeah, I'm aware of that." Aditi scrubs her hands through her hair. "Just for the record, there is no way you're actually trying to tell me you want to, like . . . see if we caught your uncle's death on camera. Right?"

Squirming a little, I decide to level with her. "Look, can I be honest?"

"That depends." Her eyes remain wide. "Is it gonna freak me out?"

"Flash's death wasn't an accident." I still don't know if I'm allowed to share this or not; we were never actually told to keep it a secret, but it feels weird sharing something that hasn't officially been made public. "At least . . . there was a witness who saw people fighting on the jetty around the time they say he went into the water."

"Okay." Aditi bobs her head and then glances over her shoulder at the doorway leading to the back of the store. "So, you're thinking maybe the footage is, like, evidence." Arching her brow again, she adds, "Totally not calling you a liar, dude, but . . . if that's true, wouldn't the cops have already come around here, looking for that stuff?"

"How do you know they haven't?"

"All right, that's fair." Aditi nods slowly. "But—and I

just know I'm gonna regret this—if the cops maybe already have it, why are you asking about it?"

"Because I don't think the cops are taking it seriously," I tell her with a sigh—and, unfortunately, this really is the truth.

If the deputies have been in touch at all since the day they told us Flash was dead, I've heard nothing about it. After our big fight, I've been mostly avoiding Dad, and when I *do* see him, he only talks about the Beachcomber. There haven't been any announcements about Ludlow's testimony—which the cops never even brought up with Paige in the first place—and I've seen neither hide nor hair of law enforcement since I started my amateur investigation. I don't know why they've been so inactive . . . but I've got a terrible feeling that it means they're still focused on Dad.

"I don't know what kind of evidence they have or don't have," I admit, fingering the corner of a laminated ad next to the cash register—for some international calling card with a list of implausibly low rates. "But I mean . . . it's my uncle, Adi. If someone killed him, I can't just sit around and wait to see if they'll get caught. If there's something on those cameras that can prove who did it, I have to know!"

"And what'll you do if there is?" She peers at me through

her fingers, like she can't bear to watch, and I can tell her real question is *What are you trying to get me involved in?*

"Obviously I'll tell the cops." I squint at her. "I'm not a vigilante, or whatever—I just want to make sure the guy who maybe *murdered my uncle* doesn't get away with it." She groans anyway, closing her fingers and pressing against her eyes. I persist, "Listen, if the cops have already seen the footage, then there's no harm, right? And if they haven't, and I find something important, I'm just helping them do their jobs better!"

"Dude . . ." She pushes her fingers back into her hair, looking at the ceiling. "You are *not* asking me to show you our security feed. I will get fired with a quickness, Zac!"

"Come on, Adi. Please?" If I thought getting down on my knees and begging would help, I'd do it. "It's my uncle we're talking about—the guy who taught me how to surf, and change a tire, and ask girls out." My eyes mist over, and to my embarrassment, my voice cracks. "I'm not asking you to do anything but let me watch a couple hours of footage that's just gonna end up getting deleted anyway."

"Oh man." She drops her forehead to the counter. "Oh man, Zac. Ugh. All right. I'm an idiot, but . . . all right." Glancing up at me, Aditi narrows her eyes. "If I lose my job over this, though, your dad has to hire me at the Beachcomber."

"Deal." It's not exactly a promise I can make, but if she helps me find something that proves Dad didn't do this, then he'll kind of owe her one. Right?

Aditi ushers me into the back room, glancing around all over the place like we're about to conduct a drug deal in a public park, and shows me a computer setup where I can access the security recordings. She explains how it works, gives me about seventy warnings not to leave any trace that I was ever here, and then goes back to the counter.

My time is running short, and I have no idea how long this is going to take, but I'm doing my best to stay optimistic. There's only one camera angled toward the jetty—taking in a wedge of the boardwalk, the top of the steps down to the sand, and the beach beyond them—and if it caught anything, it would have to have been right around midnight. Pulling up the recording from the night Flash died, I skip ahead to 11:00 p.m. and start watching in fast-forward.

Immediately, I run out of optimism. I don't know what I was thinking . . . the black-and-white images on the screen are rough and grainy already, but the storm that was raging that night makes it impossible to see anything past the railing. All that's visible is what was directly illuminated by the boardwalk's floodlights: wooden slats getting hammered by the deluge, and bits of trash flying by on the hard wind. Once every twenty minutes or so, a person flashes across the screen—but almost all of them have their heads bent against the weather, making them impossible to identify.

I don't even make it to midnight before I'm pretty much ready to give up, my heart sinking as I realize this is just another dead end. Whatever happened on the jetty that night, unless Flash and his killer walked right by the electronics store, this camera isn't going to show me anything helpful. With fifteen minutes left until my shift starts, my enthusiasm drained away, I decide to just let it play through until 1:00 a.m. and then call it quits.

And then, when the time stamp reads 12:16 a.m., I actually *do* see something.

In fast-forward, I watch a figure lumber up the stairs from the beach—lashed by the rain, swaying on his feet, looking stricken and . . . scared? I slam the pause button just as he looks back over his shoulder at whatever's behind him in the dark beyond the railing, and then let it play at regular speed as he turns toward the camera again with haunted eyes and a swollen nose.

It's Shotgun McInnes.

# ELEVEN

I don't know how I get through work that night, with Shotgun's name on the tip of my tongue. The only thing that prevents me from going straight to Dad, or even the deputies, and telling them what I've found is that . . . well, I'm still not convinced they'll listen to me. The security footage is pretty damning, as far as I'm concerned, but since the jetty isn't even visible on the screen, it's far from a smoking gun.

And I'm not convinced this town wouldn't ignore a *literal* smoking gun if they found it in the hands of Shotgun McInnes.

It's when Ruby and I are prepping the dining room the next morning, after I've had the whole night to stew over it, that I can't keep it to myself anymore. Wiping fingerprints and gross, sticky mystery smears off the front windows, I blurt, "I found proof that Shotgun was on the beach close to the jetty when Uncle Flash was killed."

*"What?"* Ruby is stuffing the napkin dispensers, and she actually knocks one off the table when she looks up at me.

"I see your 'what' and raise you a 'huh'?" Mia interjects from where she's writing out the specials of the day—New England clam chowder in a bread bowl, and panko-crusted sea bass—on the slate we keep by the host station.

Technically, this isn't Mia's job, but she showed up early and wanted to help, and I was not about to turn down the chance to (a) have fewer prep tasks to do, and (b) spend more time with the hottest girl in Barton Beach and Franklin Harbor combined.

It doesn't take me long to explain what I know—in part because I still don't know all that much. "Shotgun says he went home after leaving here that night so he could sleep off all the beer, but he was lying!"

"But . . . you couldn't see what actually happened?" Mia keeps her tone neutral, but I bristle at it anyway.

"Well, no, but that's not the point." Spritzing the window with glass cleaner, I attack the remains of someone's spilled drink. *How do you spill a drink on a window?* "The point is that he was at the actual scene of the crime, right around the time it went down, and he lied about it! There's only one good explanation, and it rhymes with 'He's guilty.'"

"I mean . . ." Mia puts a little flourish on the word "chowder," admiring her work. "There are other possible explanations. Like, he could've lied because he knew he'd be the first guy people suspected, and he was afraid it would look incriminating if he admitted to coming back to the beach that night."

"Well, he was right," I retort, "because it does."

"She has a point, Zac." Ruby pushes her glasses up her nose.

"No, she doesn't!" I toss my rag down. "Whose side are you on?"

"If you didn't see what happened on the jetty, that makes it circumstantial," she tells me in her most know-it-all tone. "That means it's suggestive but not conclus—"

"I know what it means, okay?" Putting my hands on my hips, I say, "Why is everybody coming up with excuses for him? You make it sound like lying about his alibi is proof he couldn't have done it, when we know he had it in for Flash!"

"No one's saying he *couldn't* have done it," Mia says soothingly. "And it *is* really suspicious."

Mollified, I grumble, "Thank you."

"It's just that, you know, if the deputies are already refusing to take him seriously as a suspect, they're not necessarily going to see this as a solid reason to start."

"You know, you're both forgetting something really big," Ruby tells us in a singsong way that's somehow even more know-it-all than her previous tone. She waits until we're both looking, and continues, "Even if he didn't do it, there's no way he wasn't at least a witness to what happened out there. Whatever he saw, whatever he knows, he's been keeping it to himself."

And it's on that note, as Mia and I are sort of staring at each other and wondering how we both got outsmarted by a twelve-year-old, that the door opens and a woman in a very recognizable khaki uniform lets herself into the restaurant.

"Hey, Zac, Ruby," Sheriff Leslie Seymour says to us, her voice subdued and professional. "Is your dad here?"

My back goes stiff. Sheriff Seymour isn't exactly a regular or anything, but she eats here a few times a month and just generally strives to have a visible presence in Barton Beach. She has to campaign for reelection every few years, and given Flash's celebrity status and Dad's involvement in the business community, she's gone out of her way to make friends with our family.

But she's not giving off "friendly visit" vibes right now.

As usual, Dad is in his office, and when I go get him, my mouth is dry and my stomach is unsettled. The whole way there and back, I just keep thinking, *What if she's here to arrest him?* What will Ruby and I do?

"Luke, it's good to see you," Sheriff Seymour greets him with a crisp, firm handshake. "My condolences about your brother. I wish I were here under happier circumstances, but unfortunately it's got to do with Flash's death."

"I figured." Dad stands as rigidly as the fish board on my uncle's porch—as rigidly as I feel, resuming my spot by the window. "Something's come up?"

The sheriff nods. "Your brother's autopsy was completed, and I figured I'd do you the courtesy of a face-to-face visit instead of a phone call."

"All right." Dad's face loses a little of its color. "I guess you found something, if you came out all this way."

"We did, at that." Seymour perches on the edge of a table. "We still can't be precise about time of death, but we're sticking with a range of eleven p.m. to two a.m. as our best guess." The way she says it is so clinical it makes me shudder, the thought of my uncle lying on a metal table with his chest split open like a bag of popcorn springing to mind. "He'd been drinking, but not so much that he'd have been seriously impaired."

"None of that is exactly news," Dad points out, tugging at the strap of his watch—a nervous habit of his. "Nothing worth a visit, anyway."

"You're right." She sighs. "So here's the big takeaway, Luke: There was no water in your brother's lungs."

You could hear a pin drop, and Ruby sits up straight, her eyes going wide. Dad clears his throat. "Excuse me?"

"What I'm trying to say is that Flash didn't drown, Luke.

He was dead before he hit the water that night—apparently from blunt force trauma to the skull." The sheriff draws herself upright again. "I hate to say it, but we've taken the possibility of an accident off the table. Your brother's death is officially a murder investigation now."

# TWELVE

"It was Shotgun!" I announce it without planning to, without thinking, the words just bursting out of me before Sheriff Seymour can try to lay the charge at my dad's feet instead.

"Zac," Dad begins, already angry, but I don't let him finish.

"No! You didn't see him go after Uncle Flash that night, okay? *I did*. Shotgun was totally unprovoked, and he wasn't just drunk and trying to blow off steam; he was out for blood." Urgently, I gesture at Mia, and all the heads in the room swivel her way. "Mia was there—she can back me up!"

I've put her on the spot, and I know it—and it would serve me right if she *didn't* back me up—but she lets out a breath. "I didn't see how it started, but he's not wrong about it being vicious. I've broken up fights before, and theirs was a bad one."

"Uncle Flash threatened to break Shotgun's other leg," I state. Dad flinches, and Sheriff Seymour looks at the floor. "Those were his exact words: 'Maybe I'll break your other leg tonight.' Fifteen years after—"

"*Zac!*" Dad's face is pink going on crimson, but I won't stop.

"*No.* That's what they were fighting about," I shout. "Why do we have to pretend the past never happened? They were fighting about what went down fifteen years ago, and Flash said, 'Maybe I'll break your other leg tonight,' and then Shotgun threatened to 'finish what they started.'" I'm breathing hard by the time I'm done, but at least they're all listening to me. "And then Uncle Flash turned up dead in the cove."

"All right, Zac." Sheriff Seymour folds her arms over her chest, giving me a sad look. "I hear you. Things were always ugly between those two, and maybe they'd gotten uglier in recent days . . . but, you know, my deputies did question Dustin—Shotgun—after what you said when they were here before, and they didn't get anywhere. He claims he was at home, sleeping off his booze, and we just don't have any reason to doubt it."

"I can give you one," I shoot back. "He was on the beach at quarter past midnight when Flash died—right at the jetty. There's proof."

When I explain about the security footage, Seymour's expression goes from patronizing to serious in nothing flat. After reading me the riot act for "meddling in an active investigation," the sheriff storms out—failing to let me know if she's planning to follow up on my tip or not. And when the door bangs shut behind her, I can tell by the darkening expression on Dad's face that my angry lectures have only just begun.

At the very least, Dad is thoughtful enough to drag me into his office to chew me out behind closed doors, instead of doing it in front of Mia.

"An *amateur investigation*?" he explodes, dragging his hands through his hair. "What the hell were you thinking? Just what was going through your head that, at any point, you thought that was a smart thing to do? Was anything going through your head *at all*?"

"They said they thought *you* might have wanted to kill Uncle Flash," I point out, my voice pitifully thin. "They wouldn't listen to me."

Growing up with a single parent wasn't always easy, and the restaurant was so demanding that there were weeks where Ruby and I only saw Dad on the days we had to hang out in the kitchen. But he was pretty much our whole world, and for most of my childhood, I had nightmares about something terrible happening to him, leaving me and my sister all alone. How could he expect me to sit by and watch them come true?

"When I told them Shotgun threatened Uncle Flash, they acted like it was no big deal." I blink the moisture out of my eyes, refusing to cry in front of him. "They were never going to look for proof that he was guilty if I hadn't done it for them. So you're welcome."

And then I do something I've never done before: I walk away from Dad before he's dismissed me, leaving him speechless at the audacity of it, my whole body throbbing with heat and hurt and adrenaline.

---

If I thought getting through my shift the night before was tough, tonight makes it look like a breeze by comparison. For the third night in a row, Dad all but disappears, and on the rare occasions that he's anywhere nearby, he barely even looks at me. Haley is as demanding as ever, a stack of glasses fall over and break in the kitchen, and the Spring Breakers are back in droves. It's good for business, I guess, but all of them are hungry for sordid details about "the dead guy on the beach"—clearly not aware of the connection between Flash and the Beachcomber.

What makes the hours really drag, though, is not having any clue what's happening with the cops and Shotgun. The *Gazette* has a police blotter, but no matter how many times I refresh the page, all it shows for the past twenty-four hours is one domestic disturbance and a couple of break-ins on the west side. I'm positive Sheriff Seymour believed me—enough to yell at me about butting into police business, anyway—so I have to assume she'd follow up with the electronics store. And even if it is just more circumstantial evidence, it still shows that he lied to the police about his alibi, right? And isn't that a crime itself? Either way, it has to be enough that they'd at least want to question him again.

My confrontation with Shotgun comes back to me, his blotchy, wild-eyed expression as he snarled, *I had nothing to do with his death, you got it?* He was lying, obviously, and I get angry all over again at everyone who's told me I was off base for thinking he might have done something to Flash. After the fight I witnessed, after the way he nearly lifted me off my feet with one hand . . . it's beyond clear that he had the motive, means, and opportunity—the trinity of determining guilt, according to Ruby—to kill my uncle.

When 10:00 p.m. rolls around and we've still heard nothing, I give up expecting news tonight. Frustrated and out of sorts, wondering how I'm supposed to get to sleep when Shotgun is still out there, I tie off a couple bags of kitchen trash and start for the rear exit. He knows I suspect him now, thanks to my own big mouth, and he may put two and two together if the sheriff suddenly rousts him the day after our confrontation. It's the main thing on my mind as I shoulder the door open and peer into the shadowed slice of sand behind the restaurant—knowing the guy has a history of attacking Fremont men out there.

The coast seems to be clear, though, the narrow strip empty in the moonlight. The boardwalk is crowded, a cacophony of music and chatter carrying on the breeze, and the shadows that cloak the support beams beneath it are dense but still.

Dragging the heavy bags out behind me, I start toward the dumpsters where the beachfront businesses leave their trash. And it's only when I'm right up against it, when it's way too late to turn and run for safety, that I realize one of the shadows under the boardwalk is a person.

Seated in the sand, Shotgun leans against one of the wooden pillars, facing the back of the Beachcomber. For one horrifying moment, I'm sure he's been waiting for me— that the cops hassled him and let him go, and now he's come back to give me the beating I almost got from him yester- day in the cove.

But I'm wrong. He doesn't jump me, and he doesn't call me out. He doesn't even move. Blood streaming from a half-dozen open wounds in his chest, he just sits there with his eyes open, glazed and empty, staring at me.

Shotgun McInnes is dead.

# THIRTEEN

Needless to say, the rest of the evening doesn't go so great. When I stumble back into the restaurant, the first people I tell are the cooks—because they're the first people I see. They tell Dad, and Dad tells the cops, and by the time the deputies arrive, there's no keeping it from the customers anymore.

Within fifteen minutes, the restaurant is all but empty—not technically part of the crime scene, but close enough that most people are too freaked out to stay. A handful of dedicated drinkers and locals remain, but that's it. And a muscle under Dad's eye starts to twitch as he visibly calculates all the revenue we're losing when yet another spring break night turns into a catastrophe.

The deputies who respond to the call are the same ones

who came to tell us about Flash, and the reunion is not a warm one. Chewing gum in a manner I can only describe as "aggressive," the first man grunts at me. "So tell me again how you knew to look for him under the boardwalk."

"I didn't." I'm speaking through my teeth, too agitated to control my irritation. "What I told you, a couple of times now, is that I was taking out the trash and saw him propped against one of the wooden supports. His legs were sticking out."

My statement ends in a gross noise as my throat closes up, my gorge rising unexpectedly. I've never seen a dead man before, and the vacancy in his eyes, the smell of all that blood mixed with seaweed and rotting trash, is something I'll never forget.

"What happens now?" Dad asks from where he stands behind my chair. Obviously, he couldn't exactly keep up the silent treatment after I found Shotgun, but to call the atmosphere "strained" would be generous. "You're not going to shut us down, or anything, are you? The body isn't technically on our property."

I want to give him a horrified look—like, *that's* what you're thinking about right now? But of course it is. Where I see a corpse, he sees a scarecrow standing between the Beachcomber and the tourists it needs to stay afloat. It makes me resent the place even more somehow. Like it's this beast that has to be fed, at any cost, or we'll all be sorry.

"I don't think that'll be necessary, Mr. Fremont." The deputy tucks his notepad away. "It's an ugly bit of business, but it's not hard to guess what happened here. Dollars to doughnuts, he was trying to buy something he shouldn't have, and things went south."

*"Drugs?"* I blink up at him. "Are you trying to be funny?"

"Zac." Dad doesn't even have the energy to put any real oomph into it.

"If you know something you haven't told us yet, it would be nice of you to share," the second deputy says, wearing his impatience on his sleeve. "Otherwise, I don't think we need anything more from you, son."

"You're seriously going to stand there and act like this has nothing to do with my uncle?" I'm incredulous, and although I don't actually expect Dad to back me up, it hurts when he stays quiet.

"If you know something that ties this to your uncle's death, I can't wait to hear it." The deputy crosses his arms. "Because, so far, you haven't given us much at all."

"If you need me to spell it out, then maybe you're in the wrong line of work," I shoot back. "But two surfing legends murdered on the beach within days of each other is one hell of a coincidence, yeah? Even more so when you consider that Shotgun lied about where he was when Flash got killed, and then evidence turned up—evidence *I found*, by the way—putting him right at the scene of the crime!"

"Kid, I may be in the wrong line of work, but if I go to court with 'coincidence' and 'circumstance,' I really will lose this badge." The deputy snorts. "And weren't you the one telling us all that Shotgun was the killer, and we should do our jobs and arrest him? What exactly happened here, then, according to your theory? He stabs himself six times and then hides the knife?"

My face boils, and I clench my hands until my knuckles pop. "I don't know what happened, Deputy, but my *theory* is that you suck at your job!"

"*Zac.*" This time Dad musters some enthusiasm, but I barrel ahead anyway.

"You guys refused to listen to me when I told you Shotgun was connected to my uncle's murder, and you were wrong. He was on the beach at the time it happened! He lied to you about it, and I found the proof—and now he's dead, too, and you're *still* claiming there's no connection?" I smack my head like I'm trying to get it to work. "This isn't rocket science."

"If Shotgun killed your uncle, and this is somehow connected, then who killed him? What's the conspiracy behind all this?" the deputy returns, his face going pink. "Listen to me good, son: You don't know half as much about the world as you think you do. For the record, drug sales on the beach are about as common as seagulls come spring break—we're talking coke, heroin, opioids, you name it. And Shotgun was no stranger when it came to finding dealers." Rubbing his mouth, the man sighs. "I guess it can't hurt him now to just admit the guy had a problem."

"Painkillers, mostly," the first deputy chimes in, speaking to my dad. "He developed a dependency after his injury. He managed to get clean for stretches at a time, but we picked him up more than once trying to buy pills—off college kids or whoever else he thought might be carrying. And from the looks of the crime scene . . . well, there's paraphernalia present that suggests it's exactly what it looks like."

"I know you're emotionally invested in this one, son," the second deputy says, his tone masterfully condescending, "but sometimes a cigar is just a cigar."

It takes every ounce of willpower I've got left just to bite my tongue.

_____

Dad resumes his silent treatment after that, and once we've locked up, he heads to the sheriff's station to answer yet more questions for the deputies, barely even bothering with a goodbye—which is just fine with me. Feeling betrayed by pretty much every adult I've ever known, I'm more than happy to keep my own company. Plus, I'm not exactly feeling as smart as I once did. Although I hate to admit it, the deputies were right to mock me for insisting that Shotgun was the killer, and then downgrading it to "involved" after he was killed himself.

But I don't know how else to look at it. Do people sell drugs on the beach? Of course they do—I'm not naive. But as far as I know, we only get a few drug-related deaths a season, and all of them are overdoses. There wasn't a single murder in the entire city last year, according to Sheriff Seymour's reelection campaign . . . but now we've had two in the same week? No matter what the deputy says about coincidences, I just can't accept that their deaths are unrelated.

Two surfing legends—archrivals who couldn't stay out of each other's way—brutally killed within a few days and about hundred yards of each other? And one of them after it came to light that he was at the scene of the first crime. Something else I hate to admit, though, is that *What's the conspiracy behind all this?* is a really good question.

---

"I still think Shotgun was another witness," Ruby insists the next morning. We're standing at the railing of the boardwalk, sharing a cone of french fries with Xavier and watching the waves smack into the cove. "It's the only thing that makes sense."

"None of it makes sense, Ruby Roo," Xavier says with a sigh, licking salt off his fingers.

"The killer found out someone saw him, and tried to shut him up." My sister is resolute. "It happens all the time."

"It does not 'happen all the time'!" Xavier laughs. "You

really need to get a new hobby. Don't they have podcasts about, like, arts and crafts?"

"Why didn't the killer target Ludlow, then?" I'm brooding, staring at the jetty—at what's left of the shrine to Flash, which got pretty wrecked by the tide last night. "He's the one who actually came forward with a statement. Shotgun was telling people he didn't know anything."

"Yeah, but Ludlow's story was kinda weak." Ruby crams two fries into her mouth at once, barely bothering to chew before she continues, "He didn't know what he saw, or how many guys there were, or even if Uncle Flash was for sure one of them. Besides, he went to the cops before the news was even out, so it was too late to shut him up, anyway."

"Good point." Xavier gives her an approving look and then nudges me in the ribs. "What's your theory, dude? You're being super quiet."

"I can only think of two explanations that make sense." I turn to him, shielding my eyes against the sun. It's a nice day, and if the tourists can get over the dead body behind the restaurant, it'll probably be another busy night. "Number one is that Shotgun had an accomplice—someone who helped him kill Flash and then turned on him when I found proof he was involved, because they were afraid he'd confess."

"Okay, an accomplice. I like it." Xavier bobs his head, snatching a fry out of the cone. "Like, who, for example?"

"I don't know." I hate saying it, but it's the truth. Paige barely seems upset that Flash is gone, but that doesn't necessarily mean she wanted him dead. And with Shotgun out of the running, the only other suspect I've got is the one that I won't permit myself to consider: Dad. And even if I do go there, even if I let the deputies get in my head that much, I still don't see him choosing a guy like Shotgun as his sidekick.

"You said you had a second theory," Ruby points out, unabashedly nosy.

"Shotgun was a witness, like you said." *My crap luck is finally turning around for the first time in my life*: When he'd said it, sneering at me over my uncle's memorial, I'd thought he was gloating. I thought he was trying to say that Flash's death was the first bit of good fortune he'd had in a while, and it sent my rage into the red zone. But what if he meant something else? "But maybe instead of going to the cops with what he knew, he decided to blackmail the killer. So stabbing him wasn't just about shutting him up, but neutralizing him as a threat."

"Whoa. Okay, yeah." Xavier looks out at the jetty with me. "Shotgun was just dumb enough to do something like that."

"But it still doesn't explain who the killer actually was." Ruby is quick to find the flaw in my theory. And, sadly, I have nothing to say for myself.

"No," I agree. "It doesn't."

We finish our fries, and then Xavier walks us as far as the Beachcomber, waving goodbye as he continues on toward the pier and his job at Whitecaps, while we let ourselves into the restaurant. Clam chowder is still one of the daily specials, which means we're going to spend a few hours today hollowing out bread bowls. I can hardly wait.

While Ruby heads straight for the kitchen, I decide to suck it up and let Dad know we're here. At the very least, I deserve credit for coming in early—again—even when he's barely speaking to me. The dining room is empty, but nine times out of ten these days, he's either running errands or barking at somebody on the phone. When I reach the bar, I hear noise coming from inside his office . . . but I'm not at all prepared for what I find when I push the door open.

Paige Dufresne, her hair disheveled and a cigarette clamped between her teeth, is rifling through the drawers in Dad's desk. Her face is so pale the skin is practically translucent, and her eyes are bloodshot when she snaps her head up, giving me a look that verges on feral. For a moment, we're both frozen in place, staring at each other. There are papers everywhere, the rug on the floor is askew, and the bookcase looks like it's even been pulled away from the wall.

"What the hell are you doing in here?" I ask, taken aback by the disarray—by the very fact of her presence.

"I'm looking for—" She cuts herself short, skittering her gaze around the room. "I'm looking for Flash's things, okay? You got a problem with that?"

"Yes?" I shift my weight, a disbelieving laugh coming out of me. "This is my dad's office."

"Yeah, I know where I am, thanks."

"Uncle Flash didn't keep anything in here," I elaborate, not sure what I'm supposed to do about this. "So, maybe you should just—"

"Flash kept stuff everywhere." She yanks open another drawer, rummaging through its contents, and my anxiety skyrockets. Paige shouldn't be in here, but what am I supposed to do? Wrestle her out the door?

"Stop it!" I feel like an idiot, marching across the room and shoving the drawer closed again, narrowly missing her fingers. She gives me a nasty look, turns, and just opens a different drawer. "What is wrong with you? This is my dad's desk—these are *his* things!"

"Flash was here that night; you said so." Paige is in my face so fast, I find myself up against the wall before I know I've taken a step. "Some of his stuff is missing from our place, and I need it back, okay? If your dad is keeping it somewhere, you better tell me!"

In the years I've known her, I've never considered how intimidating Paige can be, but right now, she looks like she's ready to take me to the mat . . . and I'm not sure she'd lose.

I still haven't forgotten what Flash said about her when I found him nursing his black eye: *She's got an even better left hook than the dude that gave me this.*

"I have no idea what you're talking about!" I tell her honestly. She smells like stale tobacco and nervous sweat, and there's a bruise at the base of her neck that looks like a thumbprint. She's in far worse shape than the last time we met, and her energy is pure desperation. Some gut instinct tells me it's not just grief that's causing her to unravel this way. "Dad wasn't exactly in the mood to do Flash any favors that night— and Flash was avoiding him, anyway, so they didn't even *see* each other, okay?" She takes a step back—just one, but enough for me to relax again—and I catch my breath. "Dad is gonna lose it when he sees what you did to his office, by the way."

"You think I care?" She laughs, a high, unstable sound that ends in a cough. "Do you think I'm scared of *Luke Fremont*? He's not even in my league, kiddo." Stabbing her cigarette out on the surface of his desk, leaving a scar in the wood, she adds, "That uptight mama's boy has no idea what kind of damage I'm capable of—but I'll be happy to give him a demonstration if he gets between me and what's mine."

"I just told you: Flash and Dad didn't even see each other that night!"

"And *I'm* telling *you* that they did." Abruptly, she spins away from me, striding to the bookcase. It's stocked mostly with binders and instruction manuals—stuff related to the business and all the DIY repairs we have to do—but there are lots of knickknacks scattered on the shelves as well. Photos, postcards, mementos . . . stuff like that. From the collection, Paige snatches down a seashell I've never seen before and waves it in the air triumphantly. "See? This is one of his. Proof that he came in here that night."

Before I can question the logic, she's tossing it at me, and I barely get my hands on the thing before it can hit the ground. To my shock, what I'm holding is a butterfly conch—an extremely rare species that only washes up on our coastline once in a great while. It looks ordinary from the outside, but the smooth inner lining of the aperture is astonishing. A gradient of soft blue tones, overlaid by a pattern of darker spots and bands that give it an otherworldly look. They drive collectors nuts.

Supposedly, they're worth a fortune, and she just lobbed it at me like a beanbag.

"How do you know this is his?" I'm staring at it, a million other questions racing in my head. *A seashell?*

"I just know, okay?" she says caustically. Her gaze flying around the room again, she then points at the squat fireproof safe by the wall in the corner, demanding, "What's the combination to that thing?"

"Are you kidding? You think my dad would tell me something like that?" He would, of course—he *has*. Just one of the many fun things about having a family business is that, "just in case something bad happens," I need to know how to get my hands on the title deed, the loose cash, and my father's will. But that's hardly the point. "You think if I knew it I would tell you?"

"I think if you knew what was good for you, you would, yeah." She's back in my face again, shoving at my shoulder so hard I trip over my own feet. "This isn't a game, Zac. Look in my eyes: I am not in a good place right now. Okay? I've got some serious adult problems to worry about, and I don't actually give a rip that you're only fourteen—"

"*Six*teen!"

"—I will mess you up, just the same." She's right on top of me, breathing hard, and I can tell she means it. According to Flash, Paige once sent a biker to the hospital, smashing a bottle of Jack over his head when he lost control at the Tiki Touchdown. My uncle always made it sound like this hilarious, heartwarming story about how cool his girlfriend was, but I'm starting to realize that she might be actually dangerous.

"I don't know the combination to the safe," I lie, making sure I maintain eye contact. "But if you tell me why Flash was avoiding you, and why you think he'd keep things where you couldn't find them, maybe I'll help you look."

It's in the middle of this stalemate that my dad finally makes his appearance. "What the hell is going on in here? Zac? *Paige?*"

"Where is it?" She whirls on my dad, narrowing her

eyes, and the jagged band tattooed around her upper arm ripples as she tightens her hand into a fist. "I know you saw him the other night—and don't lie to me, Luke, because I don't give three strikes."

"I assume you're talking about my brother." He looks down at her along the length of his nose, not bothering to hide his distaste. "But I don't have a clue what else you're getting at. Are you the one who trashed this place?"

"She was going through your desk—" I begin, feeling like a tattletale, and she shoots me a glare so deadly I shut my mouth again.

"You know exactly why I'm here." Paige turns back to Dad. "What'd he say to you? What did he give you?"

"The only thing my brother ever gave me was a headache," Dad retorts, stepping past her to shut the open drawers and start rearranging the surface of the desk. "And a lot of disappointment. If you want something, Paige, spell it out. And do it fast, because you've got about thirty seconds before I call the sheriff and report a theft in progress."

"I'm only here to get what's mine, Luke." She gives him a reptilian smile, not the least bit moved by his threat. "Or maybe I should say 'what's coming to me.'"

"No riddles. I don't have the patience." Dad glares at her. "Just tell me what you're here for and get out. We've got a lot of work to do—and, honestly, if there's one upside to my brother's tragic death, it's that I'll never have to see or hear from you ever again."

"That's what you think, is it?" Her smile widens, Grinch-like, her hair practically curling with malevolent intention. Leaning down, she scoops her purse off the floor near the base of the desk, whipping out a folded sheet of official-looking parchment paper. Slapping it on the desk in front of Dad, she declares, "I think you and me are gonna be spending a lot more time together. *Partner.*"

When I get a look at what the document says, my eyes go so wide they nearly fall clean out of my face.

# Certificate of
# *Marriage*

*This is to certify that*

Paige Amelia Dufresne   *and*   Christopher William Fremont

*were wed on the*   14th   *day of*   February

*by*   Thomas Stillwell, Justice of the Peace

*at*   Barton Beach City Hall

Paige Dufresne
BRIDE'S SIGNATURE

Christopher Fremont
GROOM'S SIGNATURE

OFFICIAL COPY

# FOURTEEN

Dad's face has lost all its color. "You cannot be serious."

"As a heart attack." Paige leans over the desk, enjoying herself.

"Is this real?" He runs his fingers over the embossed stamp on the page, subtly shaking his head. "He couldn't have been this reckless. He wouldn't . . . If this is real, why didn't he tell me about it?"

"Why didn't he tell his super-supportive big brother that he was marrying the girl of his dreams?" Paige counters with a saccharin look. "Maybe because he knew you'd tell him he was being stupid and impulsive and immature, and all the other crap you used to tell him, no matter what decisions he made."

Dad pushes the marriage license away, swallowing. "I cannot believe this."

"Believe it, baby." Paige snatches it up again, returning it to her purse. "Flash and I got married on Valentine's Day, which makes me Mrs. Christopher Fremont, which makes me the girl who gets everything he left behind." With a flourish, she adds, "Including his half of the Beachcomber."

*"What?"* My jaw drops, the pieces refusing to match up in my head. *Paige* owns half the restaurant now? *Is that even possible?*

"No." Dad glares at her, his tone lethal, but she only seems more amused.

"Oh, yes." She folds her arms. "We're in business, you and me, and I don't think I'm gonna take it for granted the way Flash did. I got big ideas, Luke!"

*"No,"* Dad repeats, a muscle fluttering in his jaw. "I will contest that document. My brother always got depressed during the winter months, and he made a lot of poor choices he eventually came to regret. This would've just been another one. He was probably drunk when it happened—I doubt he was in any frame of mind to sign legal paperwork, and my lawyer will—will . . ."

He trails off, horror etching lines across his face in real time, and Paige cackles. "Your lawyer will—will . . . what, Luke? Send me a card? We got married at city hall in front

157

of witnesses, including a couple guys from the Double Barrel. Flash knew exactly what he was doing—in fact, it was his idea."

"Not a chance." Dad shakes his head. "Not a chance in hell. Everyone knows how much you manipulated him. Getting this annulled will be a walk in the park."

"An expensive walk, but sure, have at it." She shrugs, lighting up another cigarette. "I'm not worried. Me and your brother were together for five whole years, so it's not like you couldn't have seen it coming. You're only surprised because you think I'm trash and you never took our relationship seriously."

They're so caught up in their conflict that they've all but forgotten I'm in the room, and it feels like I'm watching an animal attack on one of those nature channels—I can't look away. If Paige is really my aunt now, and she really owns Flash's half of the Beachcomber . . . what does that mean for us? What can she do?

"I never took your relationship seriously because you never actually cared about my brother," Dad snaps, cords rising along his neck. "Whatever reason you had for marrying him, it wasn't love. And I don't believe for a second you care about this restaurant, or what it takes to run the place, so why are you here?"

"You know what? You're right, Luke." She leans against the doorframe. "I don't really like this place all that much.

It's small and tacky, and it smells like moldy fish, and I'd probably get bored of it after a year or two." Giving my dad a minute to process the idea of two years with her as a business partner, Paige adds, "Tell you what: Why don't we make this easier on everybody, and you can just buy me out of Flash's half. That way the whole place will be all yours— just like you always wanted."

Dad's jaw shifts. "Excuse me?"

"Gimme a break." Paige rolls her eyes. "I was sitting right next to Flash two months ago when you chewed him out over the phone, telling him he didn't deserve to earn anything off his stake in the restaurant. You said he was selfish for not signing his half over to you." Smiling again, she says, "Well, you're in luck now because I'm happy to do what he wouldn't. You can just pay me . . . let's say eighty grand, and I'll have that paperwork filled out before you can blink."

"Eighty . . . eighty *grand*?" I'm surprised the back of dad's head doesn't explode. "Are you out of your mind? I don't have that kind of money!"

"You literally own property *on the beach*," she retorts, her brows coming together. "I'm sure you can figure out a way to dig up what I'm asking for. Take out a mortgage or something."

"I'm not *mortgaging my business* just to keep you away from it!" Dad slams his fist down on the desk, with so much force it knocks over the framed picture of Mom. "This is extortion. My brother hasn't even been buried yet, and already you're in here trying to wring money out of me? Get out of my office!"

"I'm not going anywhere until we have an understanding." Paige storms across the room until they're nose to nose, glaring at each other. "Your brother owned half this place, which means *I* now own half this place—and I won't be a silent partner. You've always told Flash I was trouble, but you don't have a clue how right you are." She reaches over and adjusts Dad's collar, her fingernails scraping his chest. "Eighty grand is all it'll take to get me out of your hair; otherwise, I will become the worst thing that's ever happened to you. And that's a promise. You won't even recognize this dump when I'm through."

"You can save your breath." My dad's voice is colder than the bottom of Dead Man's Cove in January. "All I've seen so far is a marriage license that may or may not be legitimate. What I haven't seen is a will—and without one, my brother's assets go into probate, and a whole bunch of lawyers will start deciding how they get divided." He pulls her hand away from his collar, forcing her to back off. "Knowing him, he probably had tons of outstanding debt to settle, and that could take months. You'll be lucky to see a single dime before next year, if he even had a dime to spare, and I will fight you every step of the way to keep the Beachcomber out of your greedy, lowlife claws."

"You're making a big mistake, not taking me up on this offer now," Paige snaps, saliva bubbling in her teeth. "This is me being nice, Luke. This is me being *reasonable*." With a twisted grin, she snarls, "It's a shame your brother's not around anymore to tell you what happens when I get *un*reasonable."

"Is that a threat?" Dad takes a step forward this time, looming over her, and my fight-or-flight instinct kicks in. This week, I've seen him angrier than I ever knew he could get . . . but I've never seen him like this. "You think because I went to college, or because I don't hang out in dive bars, I don't know how to fight dirty? Flash was a pushover compared to me—a glass jaw. You don't know who you're messing with."

"I know you're my new best friend, Lukey boy." She doesn't even blink. "Until you give me that eighty grand, I'm gonna be all over this place like white on rice. You won't even be able to wipe your butt without me popping in to make a comment."

"Get out of my office," Dad repeats, bellowing. "Get out of my restaurant! The next time you feel like talking, you go to my lawyer—and in the meantime, you better hope our paths don't cross again."

"You're going to regret this," Paige spits, but she stomps to the door anyway—slamming it open to reveal that most of the staff, including Ruby, have been standing in the bar area so they can eavesdrop. "All I've got to my name right now is a dead husband, a worthless job, and this restaurant. I'm going to spend every waking minute making you miserable until you give me what I'm owed! You've screwed with the wrong girl, and you better watch your back."

"I'm not the one who better watch out, Paige Dufresne!" Dad yells after her as she shoves past the seasonal hire bartender, stalking for the exit. "Do you hear me? You better hope you see me coming first!"

The front door bangs shut, the bells above it giving a merry tinkle, and in the dead silence that ensues, everyone in the room pretends to be looking at their phones. Dad isn't fooled for an instant.

"Well?" he demands, red-faced and breathing hard, his anger a palpable force. "Get back to work!" The people whose paychecks depend on Dad's signature hop to immediately, and he shoots an impatient look my way. "That means you, too, Zac."

"Can she do all that?" I ask instead, refusing to just let this go. It's too much to make sense of on my own. "Does that really make her a part owner of the restaurant?"

"No." Dad's answer is firm and automatic . . . but then

his shoulders sag. "I don't know. Maybe." Closing his eyes, he tilts his head back. "I cannot believe he did this to me. He couldn't even die without screwing me over one last time." His eyes snap open again. "I'm sorry, I . . . I didn't mean that. I'm just upset."

He doesn't look at the door again, though it's clear this is my cue to go. But something is bouncing around in my head—a question that Paige put there without realizing— and I can't leave until I've asked it. "Dad, do you know what Bel Mondo International is?"

His face darkens with suspicion. "Why are you asking me that?"

*Because Paige had it written down on the back of a scratch ticket, along with the sum of eighty grand*, I want to say, but I know that if I do, he'll just yell at me some more about my looking into Flash's death. At the time, when it was just a handful of words in the literal garbage, it didn't seem like it should mean anything to me. But after Paige demanded that exact amount of money from Dad—and seemed convinced she could get it—I'm starting to wonder. Why does Paige need that much money?

*Is the Beachcomber even* worth *that much?*

"I . . . I overheard Paige mention it the other day," I finally tell him, hedging my bets.

Groaning, Dad rubs his forehead. "Great. Of course she did."

"What is it, Dad?"

"It's a hotel firm." The way he says it, you'd think their main business was kidnapping children to work in a coal mine. "They're big—Fortune 500 big—with properties up and down the Eastern Seaboard, and now they're looking to expand into Barton Beach." He drops into his chair. "We've got nothing for them except the boardwalk—no spas, no fancy gyms, no high-end shopping . . . they want to build it all themselves. Bulldoze a few historic blocks of town, chase out the people who've been here for generations, and replace it all with a ritzy little resort community for the one percent."

"Is this . . . is that what Vincent Webb was here to talk to you about the other night?" There's a funny feeling in my stomach. In the back of my mind, I hear Paige's voice from when I saw her outside the Tiki Touchdown: *Stop thinking that "reliable old Luke Fremont" wouldn't hurt a fly . . . You should ask him about "the hotel thing."*

"Yeah." He starts going through the drawers, reorganizing the contents and making sure nothing is missing. Paige really did a number on the place. "They've been funneling cash into the city council and mayor's office, using 'donations' that exploit every loophole in the book, because they think they can buy the permits and ordinances they need." He laughs bitterly then and snorts, "Well, I guess I shouldn't say they *think* they can, because it's working. They're doing it."

"And you want to stop them."

"We're putting up the best fight we can." Dad squares his shoulders, seeming to remember who he is. "Mr. Webb might have a questionable reputation, but he's the biggest gun in Barton Beach, and he's not making it easy for the city government to sell voters on the idea. Anyway, if you want to know the truth?" A crafty glint flickers in his eyes. "The Beachcomber is what's really in their way."

I frown. "What do you mean?"

"Every bit of land that's potentially up for grabs to them is located behind the boardwalk. But in order to market a resort the way they want to, in order to get rich people to skip Atlantic City or Hilton Head or Fort Lauderdale and come here, they need to be able to promise a beachfront presence. And that means they need to buy one of the businesses down here on the sand, or they've got nothing truly special to show for themselves." Looking smug, Dad gives me a conspiratorial wink. "And we're the only one that fits the bill. We've got everything they need to put in a lounge or a restaurant or a bar—and you can't even imagine how much pleasure I get out of not taking their calls."

For a moment, I just kind of stare at him—at the water damage in the ceiling, the caulk peeling along the edge of the windowpane, the fusty carpeting under our feet that hasn't changed since Ruby was in diapers. "How much have they offered?"

Dad's expression sours a bit. "It doesn't matter. I've told them we're not interested."

"But how much?" I press, my brows coming together. "Eighty thousand? More?"

The number is a guess, of course, but not a particularly wild one. Now that I've got some pieces to put together, I can only think of one possible thing Paige might have to talk about with Bel Mondo International. And she had a pretty specific expectation of the restaurant's worth—or at least what she felt like she could demand for half of it.

But Dad surprises me.

"A lot more than that." He actually laughs a little. "That's a drop in the bucket, compared to what they've proposed. Zac, you've got no idea how much money these corporations have to swing around, or what they think it entitles them to. It's obscene."

He goes back to sorting his desk—gathering spilled paper clips, returning loose items to their rightful places—and the whole time I'm thinking about how Ruby is in the kitchen, wasting her spring break coring out bread bowls. How I got yelled at for wanting to take twenty minutes to talk with Ludlow instead of filling salt and pepper shakers two hours ahead of my unpaid shift. How I'm using Dad's old second-hand bike because every cent we can scrape together has to get poured back into the bottomless pit of the restaurant.

"Why *don't* we sell?" I blurt the question before I can

think better of it, feeling too righteous and indignant to anticipate the consequences.

"Save it, Zac," he says crisply, his gaze a warning. "Just get back to work."

"No, I'm serious." *Get back to work.* More toiling in that greasy, humid kitchen, under that rickety chandelier of pots and pans that's pretty much held up by rope and a prayer at this point. "If they're offering us a buttload of money, why aren't we taking it? We couldn't even afford to close the night after Uncle Flash died, because we would've gone into the red!"

"I'm not having this conversation again!" Dad exclaims. "We're not selling because we're not selling. Because some things are more important than money! I shouldn't have to explain this to you, of all people."

"Why? Because our problems don't need money?" I toss my hands up. "This whole place is falling apart! Every single day something else breaks down, and you say we'll have to 'tighten our belts' some more so we can afford to fix it. My 'college fund' fits in a mason jar, because we're struggling to cover the bills every week—"

"Don't talk to me about the bills!" Dad's face is scarlet. "Don't talk to me about responsibility! Your grandfather built this place from the ground up; it's our *legacy*, and I will not just hand it over to some corporate demolitionists so they can turn Barton Beach into another part-time playground for people with luxury credit cards and second homes," he fumes. "I don't care how much they offer, the Fremonts are here to stay!"

"Until the ceiling falls down because we can't afford to get the roof repaired," I shoot back. "Or maybe me and Ruby will just sweep up the rubble and keep serving crab cakes to drunk losers, because that's 'more important' than—"

*"That's enough, Zac."* Dad gets to his feet. "I can't believe that this is something that even needs to be clarified. If a gangster like Vincent Webb can see the value of solidarity in our community—of holding out against these . . . these *vampires* who want to ruin everything we've built here, why can't my own flesh and blood?" Simmering with rage, he goes back to the door and holds it open. "Go. Help your sister 'keep us afloat.' I've got about thirty minutes before I have to meet the deputies and answer more questions about your uncle's careless lifestyle. A stellar example, by the way, of what happens when you decide that accountability and integrity are for 'losers.'"

He slams the door behind me, and I stalk all the way to the kitchen with my head down, my face stinging with anger and shame.

# FIFTEEN

Ruby and I spend the rest of the morning slicing open sourdough rounds and scooping out their insides, the both of us brooding in silence. All the extra bread is set aside so we can use it later—for croutons or stuffing or meat loaf—because we literally can't afford to waste anything. Because every dollar we spend has to be stretched to the absolute limit, even if we're apparently sitting on a secret gold mine.

The whole time, my mood just gets worse and worse.

I've never really thought about what the future would be like without the Beachcomber, because it was just never a possibility. The restaurant has always been a permanent fixture—not just on the beach, but in our lives—and every plan we've ever made has had to accommodate it. As a kid, I probably would've been thrilled to think about this place as my family's "legacy." But I don't know how I feel about it anymore.

Maybe my dad doesn't mind all the bills and headaches and obligations that come with running a restaurant, but what if I do? What if it's not right for me? Because I already lose sleep some nights, thinking about what will happen if our fryer stops functioning completely, if a hurricane floods the kitchen, if the roof starts to leak. Uncle Flash didn't want anything to do with it; he traveled the world instead, competing in places like Australia and Hawaii. And, sure, he ended up back in Barton Beach . . . but on his own terms.

Is Dad even going to *allow* me to decide my life on my own terms?

"Does this mean that Paige is our boss now?" Ruby asks me out of nowhere, clearly having had quite a lot on her mind as well.

"I don't know what it means, Ruby Roo." I sigh, running my knife through the top of yet another ball of sourdough. "But you don't need to worry about it. Not yet, anyway." Thinking about the way she tried to strong-arm Dad, I continue, "Besides, Paige isn't actually interested in the restaurant; she just wants the money."

"How could she look at this place and think we have eighty thousand dollars sitting around?" Ruby makes a face. "Is the Beachcomber even *worth* eighty thousand dollars?"

"Apparently." I'm feeling too bitter to fill in all the blanks, but I do tell her about Bel Mondo International . . . and the scratch ticket with Paige's writing on the back. "It sounds like these hotel people are desperate to buy us out, and Dad won't budge. But Paige thinks *somebody* is going to give her that exact amount of money for Flash's half of the business."

"Do you really think she'd sell it to them?" Ruby's eyes get even wider. "The Bell Mambo people, I mean."

"Bel Mondo," I correct her, digging into the decapitated bread round with a spoon. It's actually kind of therapeutic. "And I think she absolutely would. She *will*, if she really does get control of Flash's half, and Dad doesn't come up with the money first."

Ruby has stopped working. "And then what happens?"

"That's another thing I don't know." But I can pretty much imagine it. Overnight, Dad would become business partners against his will with a predatory corporate entity looking to replace his "legacy" with a beachfront cocktail lounge for rich people. "Nothing good, I guess."

"I wonder why it's that number." Ruby looks at the half-emptied bread bowl in front of her. "What if she's already contacted the hotel people, Zac? You said she had their name written down days ago . . . it sounds like she thought of going to them before she thought of going to Dad."

"Of course she did." I roll my eyes. "Paige is a lot of things, but I don't think she's stupid. Apparently, Bel

Mondo can't wait to give their money away, but she had to figure Dad would resist."

"But if she did go to Bel Mondo and they *are* willing to pay her—and they want the Beachcomber as bad as you say they do—then why did she have to ask Dad anyway?"

"I don't know, Ruby!" I put down my bread bowl and look at her. "Maybe because she doesn't technically own anything yet. Dad said lawyers will have to sort through all the stuff Flash left behind before they can figure out who gets what, so it could be a long time before she can get money from the hotel people. Maybe she was hoping Dad would just pay her to avoid all the hassle."

"Dad loves hassle," Ruby observes.

"Yeah. Well, she didn't seem like she was firing on all cylinders." Remembering the way she looked, pale and frazzled and on edge, I start thinking out loud. "She must really need that money for some reason. What if what she was looking for in Dad's office was the title deed or, like, some paperwork confirming Flash's stake in the restaurant? That's something she could take to Bel Mondo, right?"

"Don't ask me—I'm twelve." Ruby shakes her head, but she picks up her bread and spoon again. "Did Uncle Flash have a life insurance policy? Maybe that's what she was looking for."

"You don't know about title deeds, but you know about life insurance?"

"On *Behind True Crime,* there was a case where a wife tried to hire a hitman by promising to pay him with her husband's life insurance money." She shrugs. "Turned out he was an undercover cop, though. The hitman, I mean—not the husband. Didn't go so great."

Ruby blabs on for a minute about the podcast, but I just stare at her, not listening. All I can think about is how not grief-stricken Paige has been since Flash died. How eager Bel Mondo is to get their hands on some real estate east of the boardwalk. *It's a shame your brother's not around anymore to tell you what happens when I get unreasonable.* "Ruby . . . what if Paige killed Flash for his half of the Beachcomber?"

The excitement about her favorite podcast drains from my sister's face in an instant. "Do you . . . do you think she did it?"

"I don't know, but it makes sense as a motive, right? And he wasn't even dead for two full days before she was thinking about how much money she might be able to get from Bel Mondo," I elaborate. "And that's assuming she wrote that note to herself on the back of the scratch ticket the same day I saw it. For all we know, she could've been planning it for a while. Weeks, even."

"But Uncle Flash was so, like . . . muscly." Ruby wrinkles her nose. "Do you really think Paige could have gotten him all the way out onto the jetty and killed him? The deputies said there was a fight."

"You didn't see her in Dad's office," I remark, thinking about how she basically pinned me to the wall—how she didn't so much as flinch when Dad got in her face. "She's not as big as Uncle Flash, but she's mean, and he told me she knows how to throw a punch. Plus, he was trying to avoid her that night, and today I saw these bruises on her neck, like maybe somebody tried to choke her during a struggle."

"I don't know." Ruby puts down her bread bowl again, her face ashen. "Did you see the bruises before? Like, when you talked to her after Uncle Flash died?"

"No," I admit, although it doesn't mean my theory isn't correct. "But they didn't have to come from Flash. Maybe they came from Shotgun."

"Oh." Ruby looks at the floor.

"He'd have been a perfect accomplice." I start warming up to the theory immediately. "Big, not too sharp, spoiling for a fight and hungry for revenge against Flash. Maybe she hired him to do it and then killed him to keep him quiet about it."

"Two can keep a secret if one of them is dead," Ruby whispers, her voice a little shaky. She looks up at me then, and her eyes are moist. "Zac, maybe you should stop. If Paige . . . if Paige really killed Uncle Flash *and* Shotgun, she's not going to be afraid to hurt you, too."

"Hey, you don't have to worry about me, Ruby Roo." I

look her in the eye. "I'm not trying to make enemies—and for what it's worth, she doesn't take me seriously, anyway. Nobody around here does." Finally, it's something I can use to my advantage. "But any credibility I gained with the cops by finding that security footage of Shotgun I lost when he died and my pet theory about him being the murderer went out the window. They're not going to listen to me if I call them and say I have a brilliant new theory for them to consider."

"So what are you going to do?"

*Something really stupid.* It's what I'm thinking, but for my sister's sake, I just smile encouragingly. "I'm working on it."

When we're finally done with our prep work, Dad still hasn't come back to the restaurant from the sheriff's station, and I have a few hours to kill before the evening rush starts and I launch into busboy mode. And since my bad idea is not going to get any better with age, I decide there's no time like the present to put it into effect. Ducking out the back, I race all the way home, jump on my bike, and head for the south side.

On TV, breaking into someone's place looks easy. All you need is a credit card or a set of lockpicks, and presto, you're in business. The problem for me is that (a) I don't have a credit card, (b) I don't have any lockpicks, and (c) I'm not sure how to tell if Paige and Flash's bungalow is actually empty. It's not like I can just call Paige up and say, *Where are you?*

Well, I could, but if she didn't hang up on me, she'd just lie or curse me out. And then hang up on me.

But if I want to know what's on her mind—why she needs eighty grand, for instance, or how long she's been thinking about leveraging Flash's share of the business for it—then second only to her cell phone, their bungalow is the most logical place to look. Besides, my uncle was avoiding her, and apparently also keeping something valuable where she couldn't find it; if he didn't trust her, he had to have a good reason.

When I get to their street, I chain my bike to a NO PARK-ING sign at the end of the block and then go right up onto the front porch and ring the bell. I figure if she's home, I'll just ask her point-blank what she was looking for in my dad's office—because the worst-case scenario is that she slams the door in my face. The best-case scenario would be that she just tells me and solves that particular mystery before I have to go to any trouble. But the second-best case will be that she's not home at all.

I ring and wait. Then ring again and wait again. Then I start knocking, and I call her name through the mail slot— because if she's just lying low, I want her so annoyed that she'll come tell me to get lost. But she doesn't. And when I'm finally convinced there's no one there, I creep around to the alley that runs alongside their building and find the bathroom window. This screen is just as warped as the one on the porch, and for as long as Flash lived here, it's been clinging to its frame by a thread.

It takes no effort at all to pop it free and slide open the pane; it takes maybe a little effort to hoist myself up and wriggle through, and considerable effort not to fall head-first into the tub and crack my skull on the porcelain. But I manage it—and when Paige doesn't immediately come running in with pepper spray and a baseball bat, I know for sure I'm not going to be disturbed.

It's weird being here now. Seeing Flash's razor resting on the sink, like he might still use it, smelling his aftershave in the air. The rear hallway is still plastered with pictures of him and Paige, smiling and happy. Their bedroom door is open, and for some reason, my heart hurts when I see the bed is unmade, the pillows rumpled—side by side, like two people are still sleeping there every night.

It makes me wonder what he wanted out of life, if being here truly made him happy. For a while, he wasn't just a celebrity in Barton Beach; anyone with a real interest in surfing knew the name Christopher "Flash" Fremont, and he was making enough in endorsement deals and sponsorships that he could have lived wherever he wanted. But he stayed in town, retired, and burned through the money. Did he ever look back?

"What do you think of the new digs, little man?" Flash asked me on the first day we came to see the bungalow he'd just moved into with his girlfriend. "Not too shabby, huh?"

In fact, "shabby" was exactly the word Dad had used to describe the place, but I shrugged politely. "It's cool. I like your table."

"Oh, yeah, that's Paige's." He glanced at the coffee table, a polished slab of driftwood supported by a wrought iron base. "She's got pretty good taste." This was delivered with a wink and a grin—a joking reference to himself. "It's kinda nice having actual furniture around, you know? When I was crashing with Spitfire, all we had were a couple beanbag chairs and a mattress he found on the curb. Your uncle's moving up in the world!"

This was also a joke, but I couldn't help thinking about how Dad had spent the whole ride over muttering under his breath about how it wouldn't last—how Flash would probably be sleeping on our couch again within a month. I was only twelve at the time, but moving in together still struck me as a bigger deal than that. "You're not getting married, are you?"

"What? No!" Flash was genuinely startled by the question. "We just . . . we like being together, that's all. Come on, bud, you know me: I'm a free spirit! My whole vibe is about staying loose and going with the flow. Once you get married, you don't get to flow anymore, if you know what I'm saying."

But when I took the whole place in—their shoes lined up

*inside the door, their wet suits side by side in the closet, his feet up on her coffee table—it sure didn't look like my "free-spirited" uncle would be flowing anywhere else anytime soon.*

———————

The driftwood coffee table is still right where it always was, but it strikes me as I look around the place just how cluttered it is. Paige used to be a neat freak, barking at Flash to use a coaster and put his things away, but either she gave up or she changed her tune because the living room is a total mess. The remnants of fast-food dinners decorate the couch and floor, dust is thick on the windowsill, and everywhere I look, there are teetering stacks of paper—magazines, junk mail, old bills.

A little overwhelmed, I sift through one of the smaller piles and blink at all the bright red notices that turn up on page after page reading COLLECTIONS and FINAL NOTICE. Next to the TV, a cluster of forms tell me everything I never knew to ask about horse racing, and where to find the best odds in Atlantic City; a sheet taped to the wall lists the NFL game schedule, with notes from Paige about which teams are favored to win. In the wastebasket, I find six rejected credit card applications in her name, all from different institutions. Together, they amount to a whopping six-figure sum—and they're sitting atop a bed of old scratch and lotto tickets so numerous I don't even bother trying to count them.

Dear Ms. Dufresne,

We regret to inform you that your application for issuance of a new FHF Gold Card has been declined. Our assessment of your banking history, debts, and earnings shows that you do not meet the necessary criteria at this time for a new line of credit.

You are welcome to apply again after six months from the date of this letter, and we have listed below a number of financial services we offer that may assist you in raising your credit score in the meantime.

Thank you for ~~consid~~

OVERDUE

C. 11 18 22 36 37
D. 12 22 25 28 36 39
E. 09 10 13 19 40 43
F. 05 06 19 20 28 32

THE POST
OFFICE WILL
NOT DELIVER
WITHOUT
POSTAGE

My eyebrows are all but pinned to my hairline as I take pictures with my phone, and the evidence of a serious gambling problem comes together before me. I'm starting to realize why Paige might need eighty thousand dollars so badly just now. Clearly, she's in debt, spending money she doesn't have on one "sure thing" after another to get back into the black . . . and it makes me wish I knew how Flash felt about it. He was never what Dad would deem "fiscally responsible," but being careless with your savings isn't quite the same thing as tossing it all away—and more besides—on games of chance.

Did they fight about Paige's habit? Did she pressure him to sell his stake in the Beachcomber, and did he refuse? Did she marry him on Valentine's Day solely to make sure she would inherit the one inestimably valuable thing he still had to his name?

Near the front door, only a few feet from where Paige and I spoke during my first visit after Flash's death, I find a basket of mail. More bills, more warnings I don't bother to read . . . and then what is unmistakably a card from Vincent Webb. Postmarked two days after my uncle died, it's already been opened, so I don't feel too guilty about satisfying my curiosity as to its contents. It turns out to be one of those pricey sympathy cards you can get at the store, with a whimsical picture of a lighthouse—which, given that Flash was murdered in the shadow of the beacon, seems pretty tasteless.

*Thinking of you in your time of sorrow*

Paige,

My condolences on your loss. I hope that one day you and Flash will be reunited, but in the meantime may this card keep his memory alive.

—Vincent Webb

The message is generic and uninspired, but it awakens my curiosity just the same . . . considering that when I ran into Webb on the front walk just outside this same bungalow, he told me he was here to express his sentiments on my uncle's passing. But why send a card *after* already making an in-person visit—especially if you can't think of anything more creative to add than "my condolences"?

I photograph the card, scrutinizing it and the envelope a little . . . but they have no more secrets to yield to me, and I put them both back where I found them. To my shock, twenty minutes have already flown by while I've been picking through Flash's life with Paige. Or maybe I should say Paige's life with Flash, since his presence already seems buried under hers. They're her bills, her racing forms, her clothes scattered around the bungalow; his scent still lingers, but hers dominates everywhere, a mix of hand sanitizer, cigarettes, and lavender fabric softener.

Does that mean anything? How long *had* he been avoiding her, anyway? Forget Paige's cell phone—now I want to get my hands on *his*, to see what he might have been saying to people about his new bride in the days or weeks before his death. Mentally, I make a note to myself to try the Double Barrel guys again, even though I already know Flash had mysteriously disconnected from them after that job in Franklin Harbor.

The passage of time and the motionless air start to get to me and the heat builds in the crowded room, a thin layer of sweat making my neck damp and uncomfortable. Paige could be back anytime, and all I've found so far is evidence that she's even worse at managing her money than Flash was.

Moving faster, being a little more careless, I make my first truly big discovery on a beat-up easy chair in a corner of the room—even though I don't fully recognize it as such right away. The side of a wooden box peeks out from under a pile of dirty laundry, and when I shove the mudslide of shirts and jeans and camisoles aside, I find a crate full of seashells nestled in a bed of straw. To my astonishment, they're all butterfly conchs, like the one Paige tossed at me in Dad's office, and according to the packing slip, there are fifty of them in total. *This is one of his. Proof that he came in here that night.*

## SHIP TO:

VDW DISTRIBUTION SVCS
8763 SCOFIELD AVE
FRANKLIN HARBOR, USA

| ITEM# | DESCRIPTION | QUANTITY |
|---|---|---|
| 3006848828 | Butterfly conch shell | 50 |
| | | |
| | | |
| | | |
| | | |
| | | |
| | | |
| | | |
| | | |
| | | |

Please contact Customer Service with any questions or comments.

## THANK YOU FOR YOUR BUSINESS!

I'd gotten so sidetracked by her claiming part owner-ship of the Beachcomber that I didn't even have a chance to process Paige's other comment—but it was the third time someone associated my uncle with seashells, of all things, since he died. First Ludlow, when he told me about the Spring Breaker who fought with Flash under the pier; then Freddie at the Double Barrel, who said my uncle was selling shells on the beach; and then Paige. It didn't make any sense to me then . . . but I think I'm starting to see the light, and I hear Gravy's voice again from when I dropped by the Double Barrel.

*Flash was something else. Always had some kind of a side hustle going.*

Turning a couple of the shells over and marveling at the delicate coloring and polished surface of the inner lining, I think about how much my uncle needed money and hated the nine-to-five life. There was a stretch there, when I was in middle school, where he taught surf lessons professionally—until he got bored with it. After that, it was a heel turn into odd jobs and day labor . . . with the occa-sional foray into less honest get-rich-never schemes, like palm readings for tourists and peddling hemp bracelets on the beach.

*Talk about a racket—that guy could've sold pearls to an oyster.*

I can only guess how much it cost him to buy this many

butterfly conchs, but given what Paige was throwing after horses and football teams and scratch tickets, he must have figured it was worth it to purchase in bulk and then try to resell them at a markup. There are always shell collectors on the beach, especially during the high season, and Spring Breakers are rarely here long enough to seek recompense if they realize they've been had.

As these things go, it's not the most sensible strategy for making fast money . . . but then, my uncle was notoriously bad at thinking things through. Just ask my dad.

I take some pictures of the crate—and then my phone buzzes in my hand, a text from Ruby asking where I am. With a start, I realize I only have an hour before I'm supposed to be back at the restaurant for evening prep. Wiping the sweat from my throat, I hurry for the one room I haven't searched yet: the kitchen.

It's as filthy as the rest of the place—maybe even more so. The stove and backsplash are caked with years of residue, and there's a faint whiff of rot in the air. A box of sugar cereal sits open on the tiny breakfast table against the wall, a half-empty carton of milk that was never put back in the fridge spoiling alongside it. A pot of congealed macaroni slowly returns to nature in the sink, four bananas have gone black and shrively on top of the fridge, and three giant Ziploc bags of ground coffee are open on the counter.

I make a halfhearted search of the cupboards and

drawers, turning up only the usual mix of dishes and food-
stuffs for my trouble, but it's when I take in the fridge itself
that I finally hit paydirt. It's covered with magnets, most
of which pin down the expected array of photos, postcards,
and take-out menus . . . but right in the center of the freezer
door is one tiny little telltale business card:

**GERALD SHAW**
REPRESENTATIVE

**Bel Mondo**
International Hotel Group
(302) 213-3273 *ext. 230*

My hands shaking with excitement, I take a photo of this
as well—focusing on the added extension number, scribbled
in Paige's handwriting. As far as I'm concerned, it confirms
direct contact between her and the Bel Mondo people, making it more than just a theory that she was looking to cash
in with them. What it doesn't tell me is if Shaw came to her,
or if she went to him . . . and if they first spoke before or
after my uncle died.

I'm banking on before. If Bel Mondo's been sniffing

around the Beachcomber for a while, there's no way my uncle didn't know about it, and thus no way Paige didn't know, either. If she only turned to them after he died, hoping they'd be quick to make a deal with Flash Fremont's widow, all it makes her is a crass opportunist. But if she contacted them *before* he died, and asked how much they'd pony up for a half stake in the family business . . . that would make for malice aforethought—a handy term I learned from listening to Ruby's *Behind True Crime* podcast.

It's as I'm putting these pieces together, trying to organize my next steps, that I hear footsteps on the front porch. And a key scraping in the lock.

Sprinting down the hall, I'm only just launching myself at the bathroom window when the front door bangs open. And I know Paige hears me, because her furious voice rings out just as I'm hurtling headfirst into the alley. But I don't even slow down; ducking my head, I race pell-mell for the street behind their building—and all I can do is hope that she doesn't catch a glimpse of me running away. That I don't end up like Shotgun and my uncle.

# SIXTEEN

The whole way back to the Beachcomber, my heart hammers against my ribs, my thighs burning as I push my bike faster than it's ever gone before. I keep waiting for Paige to come roaring up behind me in her truck, to run me down in the street and leave me for dead. Or maybe to back over me again, a few times, to make sure the deed is done.

I make it to work in record time, though, sweaty and shaken—adrenalized but not intercepted. The cops aren't waiting for me about a reported B&E, Dad isn't on hand with a screamy lecture about What I've Done, and I have no missed calls or texts from Paige Dufresne demanding to know why I was in her home. I appear to have gotten away scot-free.

To compound my good fortune, Mia is working tonight,

and as she, Ruby, and I prepare the dining room for the evening rush, I can't keep my mouth shut about everything I've learned. I blab it all—from the lotto tickets to the seashells to Gerald Shaw's business card. When I'm done showing them the pictures I took, I cross my fingers and hope that Mia hears the part about how daring and clever I am, and not the part where I nearly peed myself and ran away at the first sign of danger.

To my consternation, the part she hears first has to do with the animals. *"Horse racing?* What kind of Damon Runyon nonsense . . . when's the last time somebody gambled away their savings at the track outside of a 1950s movie about the mob?"

"I guess a couple weeks ago," Ruby answers astutely, setting out place mats on the indoor tables. "My favorite podcast had an episode about a man who was killed over gambling debts. They shot him and buried him in the woods, but he got found again when a dog dug up the body and brought one of his shoes home."

Mia stares at her for a moment. "Oooookay."

"Sounds to me like a good incentive to come up with the money, no matter what it takes." I look at my photos of Paige's rejected credit card applications again.

"Maybe when she realized how much your uncle's share of the restaurant could be worth, she just . . . snapped," Mia suggests.

I don't have the heart to tell her that I'm not sure Paige had to be pushed all that far to resort to murdering Flash. Despite all the photos of the happy couple in the bungalow, it's occurring to me that all I really saw of my uncle there was a razor, his surfboards, and a pillow that might just as easily have been rumpled by someone else's head.

"The real question is when she spoke to this Shaw guy at Bel Mondo." I'm back on salt-and-pepper duty, unscrewing the caps of the shakers so I can refill them. "If we can just somehow prove they talked *before* Flash died, I think I can convince Sheriff Seymour to take her seriously as a suspect."

"How can they not be taking her seriously already?" Mia gives us both an incredulous look. "It's *always* the spouse! I mean, she should be the *first* one they look into—unless she has an alibi or something."

"She doesn't," I state flatly. *I told him to get out. And then he never came home, and I thought he was teaching me a lesson, until the cops showed up.* "At least, when I asked, she made it sound like she was alone at home all night. I just . . . I don't think the cops are looking everywhere they should on this."

"What? Why not?" Mia is outraged, but Ruby and I just share an uneasy look.

Neither of us wants to mention what the deputies said to Dad on their first visit—or that they've interviewed him at least twice more, including this morning after he and I argued. According to Ruby, he came back from that appointment while I was still out, looking rattled and unhappy . . . and then left again almost immediately, without saying a word to anyone. She won't admit it, but I can see how scared she is, and I can't think of any way to comfort her that she won't see right through.

It feels like my life is falling apart, and my only shot at holding it together currently rests on a pile of used scratch tickets and a theoretical conversation with a hotel group representative—which I have no idea how to prove. Not so great.

"Okay, well, the bottom line is that we need this Shaw character to tell us when he spoke to your . . . to Paige. Right?" Mia asks, all business, apparently having read my mind. When I nod, she pulls out her phone. "Show me that business card again."

Confused, I do as she asks—and my eyes bulge when she puts her phone on speaker and starts dialing the man's number. It rings a few times, and then a woman answers. "Gerald Shaw's office."

"Hi, this is Paige Dufresne," Mia says pleasantly while Ruby and I gape at her. "I've been speaking with Mr. Shaw about a property in Barton Beach that Bel Mondo is interested in acquiring?"

"Oh, yes . . . this is to do with the resort?" the woman inquires. "I'm afraid Mr. Shaw is out at the moment, but I know that project is his top priority right now. If you'd like to leave a message, he'll be sure to call back at his earliest possible convenience."

"That may or may not be necessary . . ." Mia squinches up her face, sounding apologetic. "You see, there was a power surge at my apartment building, and I'm afraid it absolutely fried the hard drive on my computer. I lost all the records I'd been keeping about my conversations with Mr. Shaw—the amounts we discussed, the dates we spoke . . . everything, gone, just like that! Can you believe it?"

"Oh, how terrible." The woman clucks her tongue absently. "Have you tried calling one of those tech rescue services? They can work wonders, you know. Just last fall—"

"I tried." Mia cuts her off flat. "They said my machine is toast. I'll get blood from a stone before they can restore my data. And of *course* it would happen to me, right when Mr. Shaw and I were nearing an agreement on my late husband's beachfront restaurant, may he rest in peace."

"Oh. *Oh.*" The woman perks up. "The beachfront property? Oh my—well, I know he'll want to call you back. I'm so sorry about your troubles!"

"Thank you, that's very kind." Mia rolls her eyes. "But I don't want to bother him if it can be avoided. I know how busy he is." Mustering her most ingratiating tone, she adds, "He must have records of his own lying around, right? If you could just . . . you know, remind me of the basics—like, the amounts we discussed and the dates of our conversations, for example—that's all I need to know for now."

"Well . . ." The woman makes the verbal equivalent of a frown. "I'm sorry, ma'am, but I'm just not authorized to discuss open accounts or disclose sensitive information over the phone. The best I can do is confirm when you spoke to Mr. Shaw . . . maybe it'll help jog your memory until he can get in touch?"

"Yeah, sure." Mia huffs out a breath, shrugging an apology to me and Ruby.

"What did you say your name was again?"

"It's Paige Dufresne," Mia says. "That's spelled, uhh . . ." She starts making frantic gestures at us, and I scramble to pull up one of the past-due notices I photographed earlier in the day. Thrusting my phone into her hands, I'm sweaty with nerves as she reads out, "D-U-F-R-E . . ." Screwing up her brow, she mouths, *S? Really?* Then, back into the phone, "S-N-E. The *s* is silent."

For a long moment, there's no reply. Finally, just as I'm beginning to think the call was dropped, the woman comes back on the line. "Hmm, I'm so sorry, Miss Dufresne. I don't know what to tell you, but . . . I don't see your name anywhere in Mr. Shaw's book. Are you certain it was him you spoke to? We have a whole team working on the Barton Beach development, and it's possible—"

"No, no, it was definitely him!" Mia gives me an accusatory look, and I toss my hands up, shaking my head in confusion. "Can you look again? Maybe my name is spelled wrong in your system. It happens all the time—because of the whole silent-*s* situation."

"I can check, but it may take a minute."

As she's saying it, however, Ruby is making a frantic gesture of her own—holding up her left hand and tapping repeatedly at her ring finger. Finally, Mia's eyes go wide. "*Wait.* I just remembered, I probably made the appointment under my new last name! It's Fremont? With one *e*. Sorry . . . my husband and I only got married last month, and sometimes I still tell people my maiden name by accident."

Her delivery is a little weak, but if the woman suspects anything, she doesn't say. Instead, after another brief silence, she comes back with "Oh, of course, then—here we are: Fremont! I do see an in-office meeting with Mr. Shaw on February eighth. Does that ring a bell?"

"Why, yes, I think it does." Mia tries to catch my eye, but my focus is elsewhere. Paige met with Shaw a week before the wedding . . . and less than five weeks before my uncle died, leaving her his next of kin, and likely his sole benefactor. It doesn't prove premeditated murder, exactly—that she married Flash only after learning how much his stake in the Beachcomber was worth to Bel Mondo, and then killed him for it. But it's suggestive enough that the authorities will have to listen to me when I tell them. Right?

Although, it suddenly occurs to me, if she scheduled the meeting *before* she was married—

"Oh, now, wait a minute." Shaw's assistant interrupts my train of thought, her voice sharp with doubt. "I'm afraid I may have bungled things again. The name I should be looking for now is Paige Fremont, right? But it looks like Mr. Shaw's February appointment was with a *Christopher* Fremont. Would that happen to be your husband, ma'am? Ma'am?"

But all three of us are speechless, staring at one another as the penny drops at last, shock and disbelief hitting me in combination.

Uncle Flash had been planning to sell his half of the restaurant all along.

––––––

"He wouldn't do it." The second Mia disconnects, Ruby is already refusing to believe what she's heard with her own ears. "Paige probably just used his name because he was the one who owned half, and otherwise they wouldn't have agreed to see her!"

"Maybe." I wish I could sound more confident, but . . . what if it's true? It's like someone flipped a light switch I didn't know was there before, and I'm seeing things in a new way. Why did I just assume Flash wouldn't want to sell the Beachcomber? He didn't spend much time here, let alone have interest in running the place . . . and it definitely isn't a huge source of income day to day. If he needed money, and an international corporation came to town offering big bucks for an even partial stake in a restaurant exactly like ours . . . why should I believe he wouldn't at least consider it?

"No, not maybe!" Ruby glares at me. "He wouldn't. He wouldn't do it to Dad—he wouldn't do it to *us*."

"We still don't know anything for sure." Mia plays peacemaker, putting her hand on my sister's shoulder "Look, maybe Paige set the whole thing up, Flash found out, and that's why he was avoiding her."

"Maybe." It's all I can say, because I think Ruby is wrong. Our uncle would absolutely have done something like this to Dad. I can't forget what he said to Vincent Webb, right in front of the crowded dining room, the night before all this started: *Counting on Flash Fremont is a mistake. The day my brother does something to benefit this restaurant instead of himself will be the day he dies.* And as far as doing it to us goes? Well . . . I can't pretend I wasn't demanding to know why we weren't selling to Bel Mondo myself earlier in the day.

As far as what this new perspective means for my investigation, I don't know. If Flash actually wanted to sell, then killing him would only have made getting the money harder for Paige, rather than easier. It's possible Mia has a point, and that my original theory could still be true . . . but that's just speculation.

All I actually have to show for myself if I go to the cops now is evidence that Paige was in a lot of debt, and that she now stands to inherit something that could wipe her books clean. But I can't show anything to prove that Flash was standing in her way, or that she negotiated with Bel Mondo behind his back.

We're all still sitting in the dining room like that— grim and bleak, not sure how to break the silence that's formed between us—when Dad shoves through the door. Sitting up, I brace myself for his usual speech about responsibilities, and how "if there's time to lean, there's time to clean," but it doesn't come. Instead, he just blinks like he's not sure who we are for a second . . . and then hurries for his office.

It's definitely weird, and only adds to the tension in the air—and so the evening shift begins on an off note that doesn't get any better. I'm distracted the whole time, worrying at my investigation from every possible end, and I end up dropping a tub full of dishes. That fryer finally breaks down, leaving us with just one for the rest of the dinner service; the seasonal-hire bartender doesn't come back from his break and doesn't answer his phone; and a Spring Breaker gets wasted and barfs in the garden.

We're mice scurrying back and forth over a powder keg,

sensing that it could blow under us at any moment and just hoping we're out of the blast zone when it finally does.

But Barton Beach is a town the exact size of a blast zone, it turns out, and there is no getting out of its way when the moment at last arrives—when the door to the restaurant opens, and Sheriff Seymour enters, flanked by a pair of deputies. Almost as though he's been expecting them, Dad emerges from the bar area a few moments later, and they have a wordless face-off that makes my hackles rise.

Before I can say anything, though, the sheriff speaks. "Luke, I'm afraid I have to put you under arrest."

"*No.*" I'm so loud the whole room turns to look at me. "You can't do that—my dad didn't kill Uncle Flash!"

"Zac," the sheriff begins, giving me a dismayed look, but I don't let her finish.

"Did you know Paige has a gambling problem, and that she's in a buttload of debt?" I've already gotten in trouble once before for sticking my nose into this, but I can't help myself. "She married Flash, like, a *month* ago, and now he's dead and she owns half the Beachcomber—which she's already trying to sell! So—"

"*Zac.*" The sheriff repeats herself with emphasis. "We're not arresting your father for Flash's death. He's under arrest for the murder of Paige Dufresne."

# SEVENTEEN

Without thinking, I rush forward, one of the deputies moving to intercept me before I can reach my dad. Before I can . . . I don't even know what I intend to do. It's my worst nightmare, literally, and I'm reduced to nothing but instinct in a heartbeat. I struggle as hard as I can, but the deputy is about twice my size. He more or less holds me in place while Sheriff Seymour rambles off a litany I know by heart from TV—*you have the right to remain silent*—and to my horror, Dad just . . . stands there.

Looking pale and dazed, for once in his life he doesn't seem to have any fight in him. He doesn't argue, he doesn't get outraged or defiant, he doesn't tell them they've got the wrong guy. He just lets them cuff his hands behind his back in full view of our customers—in full view of a hundred cell phones in the hands of excited Spring Breakers who know they're all about to go viral. It isn't until he's halfway out the door that he finally meets my eye over the crowd of onlookers. "Call Mrs. Hughes. And take care of your sister."

And then he's gone.

———

Mrs. Hughes—Xavier's mom—is also Dad's lawyer. I make that call in a panic, and then my brain simply shuts down. I don't know what happens immediately after that, except that the restaurant closes for the night, the staff filtering uncomfortably out the door. It's another evening cut short, more lost business during one of our most critical weeks, but it's physically impossible for me to think about anything but Dad. It's like I blink, and when I open my eyes again, I'm in the back office with a shell-shocked Ruby beside me, Sheriff Seymour leaning against the desk across from us.

"Paige was found dead in her home earlier this evening," she explains to us in a voice so gentle and reasonable that it makes me feel as if I'm losing my mind. "A neighbor came over to complain about some loud music and found the door ajar. When there was no answer, he became concerned and went inside to look around. He found her body lying in the bathroom."

My memory hurtles backward, to the stuffy air in that bungalow—to footsteps on the porch, a key turning in the lock, me scrambling out the window over the tub. How long after I escaped was Paige murdered in that same room? For a moment, I think I'm going to hurl.

"Dad didn't do it," I insist through jaws that barely open, mostly just to hear someone say the words aloud. "There's no way."

"I'm sorry, Zac. For what it's worth, I'd like to not believe it myself." Sheriff Seymour keeps her tone measured. "But a man matching Luke's description was seen climbing out the bathroom window and running away down the alley."

"No—that was me!" I lurch upright so quickly that Ruby startles. "I broke into Flash's place early this afternoon, and then . . . and then Paige came home, and I had to go out through the bathroom window! Whoever your witness is, they saw *me*."

The sheriff frowns pityingly. "Zac . . ."

"I'm not making this up! I went there because I thought . . . I thought maybe Paige killed my uncle, and I wanted to look for evidence. There are tons of pictures on my phone that prove I'm telling the truth." As I babble, her face darkens with anger. "Paige had a gambling problem, and she needed money really badly! Maybe she got killed by a bookie, or—"

"*Zac.*" Sheriff Seymour narrows her eyes, going from Good Cop to Bad Cop just like that. "If you honestly want to confess to a B&E, we can have that conversation in a minute, but our witness was pretty clear about his time frame, which was evening—not early afternoon—and consistent with time of death." Folding her arms across her chest, she adds, "But maybe the talk we ought to have is about you leaving police work to the professionals, rather than blundering around town, and possibly compromising evidence vital to a series of ongoing investigations."

Chastened, all I can do is nod, my throat closing up. She's not wrong—and no matter what this witness says about the time frame, I'm sure it was me they saw. I'm the reason Dad got arrested for something he didn't do.

"A lot of people look like Dad," Ruby murmurs, her voice thin, her hands clasped so tightly in her lap her knuckles are white. She's been through so much, and it makes my heart hurt that I can't protect her from this. *Take care of your sister.* How the hell am I supposed to do that? How am I supposed to do anything besides clear off tables, open the safe, and screw stuff up?

"That may be so," the sheriff acknowledges, and in far kinder a tone than she used with me. "But we didn't arrest him based on a single witness statement. There are other factors at play. And we've already heard from a few witnesses that Ms. Dufresne came by here this morning, and that she and Luke got into a rather heated argument."

"That was just . . ." But I can't even come up with an

explanation that won't make it sound as bad as it was. "Paige broke into Dad's office and was going through his things. Of course he was angry."

"You mean like you broke into her place to go through her things?"

I can't even roll my eyes at this because I kind of walked right into it. Ruby, however, isn't going to take it lying down. "She was trying to make Dad angry. She kept threatening to mess with the restaurant if he didn't give her a ton of money—it wasn't his fault."

"It's not about fault, Ruby." Seymour sighs. "The fact is, your father threatened her, too. According to what we've been told, he said something along the lines of 'You better hope you see me coming'?" She waits for confirmation, but neither of us can bring ourselves to speak. "It's not exactly a secret around town how important the Beachcomber is to him. I understand why he was angry, but that doesn't make it okay to hurt other people."

"He didn't do it!" I insist, even though I just keep flashing back to the look on Dad's face when the sheriff arrived—how resigned he was, how it almost seemed like he was expecting her. "He got mad and said some stuff he didn't mean, okay? It happens."

"He also said the best thing your uncle could do for the restaurant was drop dead." The way she brings it up, completely matter-of-fact, makes my blood run cold.

"That's not fair." I sit up straight, glaring at her. "You can't just . . . Aren't things bad enough without you making them look worse?"

"I'm sorry, Zac." Finally, she really *does* seem sorry. "But the fact is that, recently, your dad has threatened two people who later turned up dead. We can't just ignore that, no matter much we might want to write it off as a coincidence."

"Oh, so *now* you think 'coincidences' are meaningful enough to act on," I shoot back, too upset and scared to consider how foolish it might be to smart-mouth the sheriff. "Nice to know they're suddenly back in style."

"Listen, Zac, this isn't an easy job, and I don't always take pleasure in doing it." She gives me an exasperated look. "But you don't necessarily know everything we know, okay? We're not basing our suspicions on one witness, or a couple of overheard remarks; there's a pattern of behavior we're looking at that suggests your dad was really, really angry with your uncle—and by extension, Paige—in recent days."

*I understand you got into a pretty nasty fight with Flash yourself.* That's what one of the deputies who came to tell us about my uncle's death said to Dad, shortly before he threw them out of the restaurant. At the time, I hadn't even wanted to think about it. Siblings argue sometimes, and no one gets under your skin like family; Ruby and I have shouted at each other—and so have Dad and I, come to that. So who cares if he and Flash lost their tempers and got into it?

But what if it was more serious than I allowed myself to think? What if the cops weren't ignoring Shotgun because of small-town hero worship, but because they really *did* have a stronger suspect to focus on? In my mind, I keep replaying Dad's uncharacteristically late arrival at the Beachcomber tonight, the way he reacted when he saw us all sitting there—nervous, like *we'd* just caught *him* doing something wrong.

Where was he all evening? Why didn't he tell the deputies they were making a mistake when they arrested him, the way he did when they first implied he might have had something to do with Flash's death? *What if my worst nightmare can actually still get worse?*

"If your father is innocent, then I'm sure we'll be able to clear this up quickly," Sheriff Seymour adds, the "if" blaring like a car alarm. "But for now, you need to understand that he's the primary suspect for the murders of both Paige and your uncle."

---

When the sheriff ushers us back out of the office, the restaurant is dark, and the mood sepulchral. Outside, the boardwalk clamors with life, Spring Breakers shrieking happily. The night is young for them, the pier still brightly lit, and they left all their cares back home. So did I, I guess . . . only this *is* my home, and I've got nowhere to go.

To my surprise, however, the dining room isn't empty.

Mia sits at the table closest to the bar, and she gets to her feet as we all walk in. The sheriff says a somber good-bye, and when the door closes behind her, I rub my face. My hands are shaking. "What are you still doing here? I thought everybody left."

"Everybody did." Mia hitches a shoulder, looking between me and my sister. "I thought . . . I figured you guys might need a ride. Or at least some company. Are you . . . ? Well, this is a loaded question, I guess, but are you okay?"

"Yeah," I lie automatically.

Simultaneously, Ruby whispers, "No."

"We're going to stay with my friend Xavier tonight." My eyes prickle, and I will myself not to start crying—not in front of Mia, of all people. "His mom is my dad's lawyer, but she . . . she's probably gonna be with him for a while."

For as long as it takes to book Dad, to fingerprint and question him, and . . . whatever else happens when you've been arrested for at least two murders.

"He didn't do it." Ruby says it to the floor. "On my podcast, there was a case where a guy in Chicago was convicted of a murder he didn't commit, and this private detective named Michelle Gray proved he was innocent. Maybe she can help us?"

"We can't afford a private detective, Ruby Roo." I'm hoarse with despair, and I clear my throat. "We can't even afford to be closed right now."

"What happens if the restaurant folds?" Mia asks, her cheeks coloring a bit as she realizes how blunt the question is. "Sorry . . . I just mean, I know spring break is huge for you guys, and you really count on the money you bring in. Between the weather and the murders, you must've lost a lot of potential revenue this week, right?"

"Yeah," I acknowledge, looking around. "I don't know how much, but . . . lately it seems like any amount is too much, according to Dad."

"So what happens if business gets so bad you have to close?" she presses. "I mean . . . you'd kind of be in a position where you'd *have* to sell. Right? And you couldn't afford to be picky about offers."

What she's saying finally hits me. "You think *Bel Mondo* is behind this?"

"Why not? They want the Beachcomber, but your dad won't yield . . . and now he may not have a choice. If there are potential millions of dollars on the line, and they've already sunk cash into the city trying to get what they want, what's a little murder?"

"But why not kill Dad, then?" Ruby wrinkles her nose, and I'm amazed again by what fazes her and what doesn't. "Wouldn't that have been easier than framing him?"

"Especially since Uncle Flash didn't want to run the restaurant anyway," I add, stepping delicately around the fact that he may have even been looking into selling his half to them already. "And Paige was almost definitely interested in playing ball with them."

"Yeah. Yeah, I suppose that makes sense." Mia leans against a table, letting out a troubled sigh. "So . . . what are you going to do now?"

"I guess we're going to Xavier's house and waiting for Mrs. Hughes to get home." I pretend to look around so they won't see the hopelessness in my eyes. "There was a witness who saw someone leave through the bathroom window at Paige and Flash's place, and maybe . . . maybe she can help me figure how I can prove it was me and not Dad."

"That's *it*?" Ruby shocks me by finally getting good and mad. "That's all? And if the cops decide to ignore you—*again*, like every other time you've tried to tell them something—then what? You're just . . . giving up?"

"Ruby!" I actually laugh a little, surprised by her fury.

"You said you were going to try and find out who really did it." A tear slips down her cheek. "You can't just quit. If we can't afford a detective, and you give up, how are we supposed to save Dad?" Then, more tears coming, her voice tiny, she asks, "What's going to happen to us if he goes to jail?"

It hits me like a fist to the gut because it's the same question I've been asking myself since the deputies first implied Dad could have been Flash's killer—and I still don't know the answer.

All I'm sure of is that we can't afford to find out.

# EIGHTEEN

If my sister is trying to guilt-trip me with her tears, it works like a charm. Asking Mia if she'll watch Ruby for a little while, I go for my bike, deciding it's time for me to confront my fears once and for all. With both of my main suspects dead, and my dad headed for the lockup, I need to know just what it is that the sheriff has on him. I need to know how I'm supposed to start fighting back.

*You two got into a shouting match two weeks ago right outside O'Malley's Pub*—that's what the deputy said to Dad when they first hinted that he was the one who killed Flash. Located on the north side of town, O'Malley's is a cleanish dive where the cops tend to gather in their off-hours. It's also close to the bank where we keep the Beachcomber's accounts, which might explain what he was doing over there. And if my father ran into Flash right after dealing with money issues, I can also understand why he might have been in the mood for conflict.

It's late, and although the pub isn't in one of the touristy areas, it's still fairly popular. But, again, lucky for me, the townie rule is very much in effect, and the bouncer turns out to be one of the many locals who live to surf. He's not someone I know personally, but that doesn't matter. My uncle knew everyone, and everyone knew my uncle—and Barton Beach is a small enough place that any surfer worth his salt will recognize me from all the time I spent with him on the water.

The guy winces when he sees me coming. "Uh, listen, dude, I'm sorry for your loss, and I hate to be that guy, but . . . I don't think you're old enough to get in here."

"It's cool—I don't need to go in." My hands are jittering so bad I have to stuff them in my pockets, the air quickly growing too uncomfortable to breathe. I don't want to be here; I don't want to know what I came to find out. "I just need . . . Is there anyone around tonight who was working two weeks ago? Who might've overheard a fight between . . . between my dad and my uncle?"

He wants to send me home, I can tell; but I can also tell when something in my face breaks his resolve. I don't know what I look like, but I feel about as wretched and pitiful as can be, and the guy is sorry enough for what he sees that he agrees to go check.

Ten minutes later, I'm talking to a bartender out back— a woman named Mae who's old enough to be my grandma and who, judging by her accent, might be the O'Malley the pub is named after.

"I was working that day, sure enough," she confirms uneasily, lighting a cigarette. It's her excuse for taking a break to speak with me, so I can't complain. "Your uncle was waiting for someone outside, I think, though he stepped in briefly to use the restroom and have a quick drink in the meantime. That's how come I recognized his voice later when . . . well, when they got into it."

"Are you absolutely sure it was my dad with him?"

"Yeah, that I am." Mae lets out an unhappy sigh. "You know, working in a place like this, I normally make a point to mind my own business. But when it came to Flash . . . well, I suppose he felt like everyone's business, didn't he? Anyway, when the two of 'em started going hammer and tongs at each other just out front there, I went to see what was up. Luke doesn't come around as much as his brother does— *did*, I suppose—but it was him all right."

"What were they saying?" I finally ask when she doesn't go any further.

"Well." She frowns at me. "Are you sure you want to

hear this? You can't un-hear it, you know." When I force myself to nod, she nods back. "Okay. I guess your uncle thought they ought to sell the Beachcomber, because he was shouting about it being a money pit and an 'albatross around their necks'—his words, mind you, not mine—and your father . . . well, to say he disagreed would be putting it mildly."

Again, all I can do is nod—because this is precisely what I was afraid of hearing. From the minute Gerald Shaw's assistant told us the appointment was made in my uncle's name, this was the puzzle piece I dreaded I would come to find.

"I've known both of them since they were small," Mae continues, speaking faster as she reads my discomfort, "and Luke was always the more serious of the two. He was the apple of your grandfather's eye, and he wanted to live up to the man's expectations, but Flash marched to the beat of his own drum, and they just saw things differently. Flash had gotten an offer on his half of the business, and he wanted to take it—said he wanted to 'get out from under' for once. He said Luke was still trying to impress their father when the man was long since dead, and that it was . . . pathetic." Swiftly, she adds, "His word, again."

My stomach somewhere down between my ankles, I swallow. "And what did my dad say?"

"Well. He called your uncle disloyal, among other

things. Said he was lazy and irresponsible, didn't know what an honest day of work was like . . . Luke said he'd put his heart and soul into that restaurant, into preserving the family business, and that it'd be sold over his dead body. And then . . ." Mae shuts her mouth. Pulling out a second cigarette, she lights it off the embers of the first, taking a long drag to fortify herself before continuing. "His final words before he stormed off were, 'You're no brother of mine. You're dead to me, and I'd rather *see* you dead than let you do this to us.'"

I open my mouth to say something, but my stomach gives one final twist, and I end up puking on the grease-stained pavement at my feet.

It's not the kind of news I can share with Ruby. When I get back to the Beachcomber again, woozy with fatigue and despair, all I manage to tell her is that it's bad. Her words from earlier hang over me like a dark cloud—*you can't just quit*—but at this point, I'm not sure what other option I have. I'm not even sure it's a good idea for me to keep trying; I've spent the past week digging into the mystery of my uncle's death, and all I've succeeded in doing is help to bury my father.

I'm the one who told him Shotgun was a possible witness to Flash's murder . . . and that same day, the guy turned up dead behind the restaurant, less than twenty yards from our back door. My reckless exit through Paige's bathroom window may be the very reason he was arrested for whatever's happened to her. And my attempts to prove *she* may have killed my uncle only turned up evidence that my *dad* was the one with a motive—and a history of threatening violence.

Mia drives us to Xavier's house, but neither Ruby nor I are able to maintain any kind of conversation. When we get there, my best friend greets us awkwardly . . . and then we all sit in silence, waiting for his mom to come back from the police station. Waiting to find out when—or perhaps *if*—my father will ever come back himself.

Eventually, we doze off, but when Mrs. Hughes does finally return, in the middle of the night, I'm wide awake the instant I hear the door open. We end up in the kitchen together, speaking quietly over hot cocoa.

"Obviously, your father says he's innocent," Mrs. Hughes begins, holding my gaze with her own. "So far, I haven't seen any hard evidence to support the charges against him—aside from the one vague witness statement—which is encouraging—but it doesn't necessarily mean our job will be an easy one. For as little as they've shown to prove their claims, we have even less to *dis*prove them."

"I'm the one their witness saw." I try again, adamant. "I broke into the bungalow looking for dirt on Paige, and I had to leave through the bathroom window. I'll swear to it—I'll even take a lie detector test!"

"Let's revisit that later." She places a hand over mine, giving me a warm smile. "If you're the one they saw, it shouldn't be too hard to break the witness's statement—no matter how much you and your father look alike. But I don't think he wants you involved in this, should it actually proceed to trial."

"Well, too bad." Dad's not the only one who can put his foot down. "If I can help, I'm going to."

"Like I said, we'll cross that bridge when we get there." Mrs. Hughes bites her lip. "The real issue is that your father *did* go to Paige's tonight. He called her several times throughout the afternoon with no answer—all of which the police will know from one look at her phone—and then he finally decided to confront her in person. He even sent her a text telling her he was coming over, so things look pretty bad with or without that witness's claims."

"Why would he want to see her so badly? Was it about what happened at the Beachcomber?"

"Yes. Your dad was hoping he could talk Paige out of what she was threatening to do," Mrs. Hughes explains. "But he says the door came ajar when he knocked. Apparently, there was loud music playing inside, and no one answered when he called out, so he got spooked and left without going any farther than the entryway."

"Then you just need to describe what I was wearing to

this supposed 'witness' and see if it matches the person they saw climbing out of the bathroom window—"

"Zac." She puts her hand on mine again and says, kindly but firmly, "I know how to do my job, okay? I'm not worried about the witness—at least, not yet. Right now, we've got two much bigger problems."

My stomach rolls again, and I nudge the cocoa away from me. "What problems?"

"The first is that your father doesn't actually have an alibi for any of the murders. When Flash was killed, Luke was alone at the Beachcomber—which, not that it matters all that much, is walking distance from the jetty. He actually went to Paige's bungalow and left his fingerprints inside the entryway, so even if I can break that witness statement, it hardly gets him off the hook." She grimaces. "And it won't look great for him that his first call after leaving there was to me. He was trying to cover his bases, describing how he'd found the place and was seeking my advice, but the sheriff may spin it differently."

"What about Shotgun?" My head throbs; this is another question I don't particularly want the answer to. "Are they still saying it was a drug deal gone wrong?"

"They aren't charging him with Shotgun's death . . . yet." Mrs. Hughes rotates her mug in her hands. "But in time, I think they will—or they'll use the implications of it to suggest to a jury that your father may be even guiltier than he appears. After all, it was a busy night, and by his own account, no one had their eyes on him the whole time. It wouldn't have taken long to pop out for a prearranged rendezvous, kill the man, and return."

"With no bloodstains," I point out, speaking through my teeth again.

Mrs. Hughes shrugs. "If they don't charge him, they don't have to worry about inconsistencies. They just have to make it sound possible."

"How convenient." The aftertaste of bile stings in my throat again. "You said there were two big problems."

"Right. The trial, if it goes that far, will be a ways off— so we've got some time to work on how we'll handle your father's lack of an alibi. The more pressing complication is how we're going to get him out of jail in the meantime." Mrs. Hughes sits up a little straighter. "I'm reasonably confident I can get the judge to set bail, but the prosecutor is pushing for two counts of first-degree murder, so the bail amount is likely to be . . . high."

My headache gets instantly worse. "How high?"

"Let's just say we'll be lucky if it's low enough that he can cover it by putting the restaurant up for collateral. Otherwise, we're looking at mortgaging the business and still trying to find additional money elsewhere." Mrs. Hughes massages her own temples. "And as far as I understand it, you're fresh out of wealthy relatives to pitch in."

"Hard to run out of something you never had." I try to smile, but those muscles don't seem to work anymore. Suddenly more exhausted than I've felt in days—possibly months—I say, "But I think I know someone we can ask for help."

# NINETEEN

Bright and early the next morning, wearing the nicest clothes I had in my closet—the shirt and pants I got for homecoming this past winter, plus a tie of my dad's that Mrs. Hughes had to help me with—I'm walking past the Beachcomber and heading for the pier. The Spring Breakers are already out in force, the air scented with ocean spray, rotting kelp, and fried food. The Ferris wheel turns slowly, and Whitecaps gleams like the city on the hill.

*If a gangster like Vincent Webb can see the value of solidarity in our community . . . why can't my own flesh and blood?* It's almost embarrassing to admit that it took me until my conversation with Mrs. Hughes to realize that when Dad said that, he was referring to Uncle Flash as much as he was to me. Actually, I'm starting to view a lot of his angry outbursts from the past couple weeks with a new perspective.

Dad and I might not always see eye to eye, and I don't really know if I understand why he's so committed to keeping the Beachcomber afloat when it feels like the struggle only gets harder every year. But I do know he *is* committed to it. I know that it gets him up in the morning, and he doesn't hate it the way I think I would if I were in his shoes—if the buck stopped with me, and there was an eternal shortage of bucks to go around.

That my uncle didn't care to work at the restaurant frustrated Dad and made him resentful . . . but I can understand why he felt betrayed when his own brother made moves to sell half of it out from under him. Flash dedicated his life to surfing, and he achieved pretty much everything he could—everything he desired, save for a handful of titles that might've made the difference between just being a local hero and being the next Kelly Slater. He got what he wanted and quit on his own terms.

But there was nothing for Dad to "achieve" with the Beachcomber, besides just keeping it going. That's all he's wanted, and it's been enough for him. Even if I don't get it, Dad's been living his dream, too. And Flash, who got admiration and celebrity and a life free from obligation, decided to just . . . take that dream away from him. Maybe he wanted to sell so he could pay off Paige's gambling debts, or maybe he simply wanted to recapture the comfort of the life he had when the winnings and sponsorships were reliably rolling in. I don't know. Maybe I never will—and maybe I don't care.

The bleak thoughts follow me all the way to the end of the pier, where I take a deep breath and will them to retreat. I need to get my head in the game.

"Welcome to Whitecaps," the hostess says, smiling ear to ear when I push through the doors. It's not very hot today, but it is humid and the change between the heavy air outside and this climate-controlled glass box just about makes my ears pop. "How many in your party?"

"I'm, uh . . ." I cough, a little overwhelmed by the opulence of the place. "I'm here to see, uh . . . to see Vincent Webb? I made an appointment."

She looks at me like I'm definitely a scammer—and I can't exactly blame her. This place serves caviar and actual champagne *from France*, and I'm a scruffy teenager wearing a necktie that belongs to a man currently behind bars for murder. "If you give me your name, I'll have someone see if he's available."

The look on her face says I've got better odds of taking a rowboat to the moon, but I give my name anyway and then sit down in a chair that's nicer than any of the furniture in either the Beachcomber or our home. Honestly, Whitecaps might as well be on a different planet than the rest of the town. Three narrowing tiers of floor-to-ceiling windows offer a panoramic view of the ocean and the coastline, and the servers wear all black and correctly pronounce things like "vichyssoise" and "bouillabaisse." There's a piano, some glass sculptures, and even a ten-foot-high aquarium that has tiny little sharks inside it.

There is literally nothing like this place anywhere else in Barton Beach, and I'm equal parts awed and intimidated. I've only been in here twice before—once when I was really little and my grandpa was still alive, and then again in fifth grade, as Xavier's guest for a birthday dinner with his family. On both occasions, what stuck in my mind is how immaculate everything looked, how refined, compared with what I was used to. I was out of my element, and I was sure anyone who looked at me could tell.

Also speaking highly of the joint: I don't have to wait long. The hostess makes a call over an internal line, and within a minute, there's an answer. Appearing startled, if not chastened, she turns to me. "Mr. Webb will be happy to see you, Mr. Fremont."

<hr>

In addition to his wealth, and corresponding influence in Barton Beach, what I know about Vincent Webb is that he doesn't want the Bel Mondo resort to break ground here. Whitecaps is the only fine-dining restaurant within about a fifteen-mile radius, which translates to a fair amount of business—and he'd like to keep it that way. I don't know if he actually cares about the little guy, or "solidarity in the community," or any of the rest of the stuff my dad said, but he wants the Beachcomber to stay where it is. And that makes him an ally, if not exactly a friend.

Now all I have to do is convince *him* of it, and I'm in business.

"Zac, come on in," Mr. Webb says when a waiter escorts me to his office. Located at the back of the restaurant, filled with modern furniture and nautical bric-a-brac, it's a sharp contrast to the stuffy little workspace my dad keeps at our place. In fact, through those ubiquitous windows behind him, I can see clear to the Beachcomber, the jetty, and Dead Man's Cove behind it. "I heard about your father's arrest last night, and I can't tell you how sorry I am for you and Ruby. To think what you're going through right now . . . it's awful. Just awful."

"Um, thank you." I sit down awkwardly in the chair across from him, a chrome frame with leather strapped across the back and seat. I've never been on a job interview before, but that's what this feels like.

"I was going to drop by today to see if there's anything I can do for you kids. How are you two holding up?"

"We're not doing all that great, to be honest." I tug at the end of my necktie, willing my voice to remain steady. Ruby basically cried herself to sleep last night, sniffling quietly until she finally dropped off. "There's just . . . It's so much to deal with. My dad is innocent, Mr. Webb—I know it—but if they put him on trial . . ."

My throat closes before I can finish the sentence, and Webb nods understandingly. "Of course he's innocent. I've known Luke a long time; he's an honest man, and there's just no way he could do something like this. Trust me, he's got the community's support, and I'm sure things'll be cleared up soon."

"The sheriff has known him for a long time, too, and she thinks he's guilty."

"Sheriff Seymour means well, but she doesn't have a lot of experience running murder investigations." Mr. Webb sits back. He isn't wearing a tie, but his loudly-patterned silk shirt looks more expensive than my entire wardrobe. "Three deaths in a week make people scared, and she's trying to show that she's on top of it. But Monique Hughes is representing your dad, right? She's a top-notch attorney; I'm sure she'll find the holes in their case."

I give a glum nod because I don't know what to say to this. I can't bring myself to explain just how bad it looks for my dad—and how maybe I lied when I said he was innocent. Because I've had all night to think about how angry he's been, about the threats that he made. Would he actually kill someone, *three* someones, to hold on to the restaurant? I don't know. And, frankly, it scares me that I don't.

Late last night, with my two main suspects dead, I finally reconsidered the possibility that Bel Mondo is the guilty party . . . and then dismissed them again for the same reasons as the first time. They want the Beachcomber, and Flash was the hand willing to feed them. It makes no sense for them to eliminate first him and then also Paige, even if they were hoping my dad would eventually take the fall for it. As a theory, it leaves too much to chance.

Briefly, I even entertained the notion that Vincent Webb might have been behind the killings; his name has turned up often enough that I had to wonder. He wants to protect the Beachcomber—and by extension, Whitecaps—possibly as much as my dad does, but I can't quite connect those dots. The truth is that, even with a resort as competition, he'd be in no real financial danger. Even if his restaurant did less business, he has his motels, and his souvenir stands would draw money from the fancy hotel crowd. Besides, the city council still hasn't approved the ordinances Bel Mondo needs before their plans can be greenlit.

It leaves me with two possibilities, the first of which is that the deaths are all unrelated: that they were killed by three different people for three different reasons. But that strains credibility to the breaking point. Barton Beach hasn't had a murder in over a year, and now it has three in one week—my uncle, his wife, and his archrival—and none of them have anything to do with one another?

But that leaves only one other candidate: Dad. He had motive and opportunity to kill all three of them—and even if the inheritance wasn't settled, Paige was threatening to destabilize something he'd ostensibly already killed for twice already. And all I've got to gainsay his guilt is that . . . he's my dad. And I just don't want to believe he could do it.

"I know Mrs. Hughes will do her best, but it's more than just that. Ruby and I are on our own now, until Dad makes bail—and that's if they even *grant* bail! Because if they don't . . . we're still minors, and they're not going to let us just crash with Mrs. Hughes and her family for months and months. What if they put us in foster care? What if they split us up?" I'm babbling, tears stinging my eyes, all my organized arguments flying out the window on a wave of despair. I'd planned this visit carefully, made a list of all the things I'd say to persuade him, but now I can't remember any of it. "And then there's the restaurant. I mean, we can't afford to be closed, especially right now, but there's nobody to run it. And we'll probably have to mortgage the property or maybe even sell it just to cover Dad's legal expenses, and—"

"Whoa, whoa, whoa!" Mr. Webb holds up his hands in a placating gesture. "Don't panic, buddy—we're not going to let any of that happen, okay? I meant it when I said your dad's got the community's support, and that includes mine." He gets out from behind the desk, circling around it and grabbing a box of tissues that he places in my hands. "Let's see what happens at the bail hearing, but I'll be glad to help you cover the costs."

"Do you mean that?" Gazing up at him through blurry eyes, I try to look adequately grateful—but I've never had to ask for something this big before. I've never had to be this appreciative. "Really?"

"You bet. It won't be a gift, exactly—we'll call it a loan—but I'm sure we can work something out." He gives me that shark-toothed smile again, the one that makes me feel like I'm being sold something I should question the value of. "This town wouldn't be the same without the Beachcomber, and it wouldn't be the same without Luke Fremont, either. He's a stand-up guy, and we need more like him."

"Thank you." I bob my head, wiping my eyes with one of Webb's tissues.

"I hope you don't mind me saying it, because I know how people looked up to Flash, but Luke's always been worth two of his brother." Webb glances out the window, at the waves rolling into the beach—at the cove surging behind the jetty. "You're lucky to have a man like that as your father, Zac."

"I thought you liked Flash," I blurt, a little surprised by his tone—especially considering how many different ways he expressed his sympathies to Paige for her loss. The day my uncle died, Webb even called him a hero to the community.

"I did like your uncle. Chris was a lot of fun—he was easy to get along with, and he made people proud to say they were from Barton Beach. All of that is important." His smile diminishes, turning apologetic. "But he wasn't reliable, and sometimes he took advantage of the respect people had for him. Your dad's not as flamboyant as his brother was, but he's a better role model. I hope you see that."

Again, I nod, because he's not exactly inviting conversation. It's a weird thing to say to somebody who's still in mourning—still in shock, honestly—but I'm essentially here on bended knee, so I'm not going to backtalk, either. I know my uncle had character flaws, but is this really the time to talk about them?

"Dad's worked really hard to provide for us," is all I come up with to say.

"And we'll work just as hard to help him out." Webb claps me on the shoulder, and for the first time, I notice sweat stains under the arms of his expensive shirt. "Let's talk again after the bail hearing, but until then, focus on your sister and let me worry about the money. We'll get him out, and your family will stay together—and in the meantime, I'll lend you one of my shift managers to keep an eye on things at the Beachcomber until Luke comes back."

"What?" This wasn't something I expected. "You don't have to do that—"

"Not a problem." He holds up his hands again. "Your dad can't afford to close the Beachcomber until this mess is sorted out—and to be honest, keeping your doors open is good for my business, too."

"But . . ." My face goes hot. "I mean, Mr. Webb . . . I really don't think we can afford to pay someone what they'd be used to making at Whitecaps. We've kind of been struggling a little."

I hope it's okay for me to say that much. Dad doesn't like us to talk about the restaurant's finances with other people, but . . . what else am I supposed to do? Never in my life did I think I'd be *in charge of the Beachcomber* before I even finished high school. A fresh wave of panic washes over me as I think about just how far out of my depth I am.

"Don't worry about it," Webb tells me. "He'll be on my payroll the whole time, all right? I can afford it. The one thing I can't afford is for those lowlifes from the hotel group to smell blood and start circling. Your dad's in trouble right now, and they'll take advantage of that any way they can. We local business owners need to stick together."

"Th-thank you," I say, startled—more than a little humbled. And yet.

It's unbelievably generous, a gift horse I can in no way afford to look in the mouth . . . but I can't shake a weird sense of foreboding at having gotten what I wanted so easily. Not to mention the fact that it's a little patronizing the way he says "we"—as if Whitecaps is just another hardscrabble mom-and-pop shop fighting The Man. Like they don't have an *actual shark tank* in their dining room, just for atmosphere. Like Webb doesn't own half the town.

Maybe I ought to say no. I came in here planning to beg, and now he's handing me more than I ever dreamed I could hope for, and on a silver platter. No questions asked . . . but not, I notice, expressly without strings attached. And if there's one thing entrepreneurs have in common around here—be they international hoteliers, shady businessmen, or self-employed ex-surfers—it's exploiting their influence.

*You don't want Vincent Webb in your business any more than the cops.* That's what Paige told me. The problem is that I have literally nowhere else to turn. Short of starting a GoFundMe, which could take forever and *still* not add up to what I'd need to cover the unfathomable debts we're about to accrue, Vincent Webb is my only hope. But when he finally reveals the strings, what will they be?

And how badly will I regret being too desperate to ask about them now?

# TWENTY

Despite my misgivings about his offer, I just thank Vincent Webb profusely and decide to leave before he can change his mind. Bowing and scraping my way to the door, I don't start breathing again until I'm back in the main room—light pouring through the windows and scattered everywhere by genuine crystal glassware. Reflections from the fish tank ripple at my feet, making the whole experience feel like a dream. A crushing weight is off my chest for the first time since my dad was taken into custody, and it's an indescribable relief.

"Hey, man, how'd it go?" Xavier's appearance at my left elbow is so sudden it makes me jump, even though I knew he'd be working today. Whitecaps does a breakfast service, and he's in the spotless black attire required of all the waitstaff here. "Is Mr. Webb gonna come through for your dad?"

"Yeah." I gulp down some more air, my face tingling. "Yeah, he is. He's going to help us cover the bail, and he's going to loan us someone to manage the Beachcomber until . . ."

I can't bring myself to say *until Dad gets out*, because I don't want to jinx anything, but Xavier gets it.

"Dude—that's amazing! I knew he was cool with Luke, but I had no idea he was so cool about, like, money." A little quieter, he adds, "My mom always says there's no ethical way to get the kind of rich Mr. Webb is . . . especially in a town as small as this."

"Honestly, right now, I don't give a crap about his ethics," I say, being mostly sincere. If he's got the cash to help my dad, and he's willing to share it, I don't care where it came from or how he got it. What I care about is what he might someday expect in return. After all, no matter how nice his clothes are, no matter how bright his smile, I can't forget that my own dad called him a "gangster."

Taking a look around, though, I decide to just drink in the luxury of Barton Beach's finest restaurant—to let go of my apprehensions, at least for the afternoon. I'm approximately 50 percent less terrified for the future, and if my family gets through all of this, we can face whatever comes next together.

If the decor of Whitecaps has a theme, it's *money*. The linens are starched, the napkins are slick, and the silverware is polished to a high shine. There are plants everywhere, chandeliers glittering in this corner and that, and the music of a string quartet plays over hidden speakers—some temporary ambience until the live pianist can take the stage. Each table is set with candles and an elaborate centerpiece of spiky coastal grasses, the green shoots rising from wide, shallow bowls filled with sand and bordered by seashells.

And not just any seashells, either, I realize. My gaze zeroes in on the nearest cluster of them—on the delicate blue gradient of their inner linings, overlaid by darker spots and bands that give them an exotic quality. They're butterfly conchs—all of them.

Turning slowly around, I realize that there's at least two or three conch shells on each table, plus others decorating the bar and the piano. There are even more at the bottom of the aquarium, resting among stones and sea glass and lesser shells, fronds of seaweed undulating around them. I've never seen so many in one place before; at a glance, it has to be at least four times what was in the crate at Flash and Paige's bungalow, and I'm stunned that enough of them exist *at all* to be acquired in quantities like this.

"I thought these shells were supposed to be super rare." I'm thinking out loud, but Xavier follows my gaze around the room.

"I know, right? It's wild." He shakes his head. "There's got to be over a hundred on the tables, alone. People walk out with them, too, and the managers don't even get mad about it. They just go in the back and replace them."

"Replace them?" I squint at him. "How many do they have?"

"There's, like, two full crates of them in the storeroom!" Xavier tosses his hands out. "They just sit there between the soy sauce and the napkin rings, like it's normal. Rich people don't make any sense."

But I miss the last part of what he's saying, because in my mind I'm suddenly back in my uncle's bungalow, shoving aside a pile of dirty clothes to uncover a wooden crate full of priceless seashells. Not sure what it means—or if it means anything—I ask, "Can I see?"

Xavier gives me a weird look but shrugs his consent. Checking to make sure the coast is clear, he leads me into the kitchen and shows me the dry storage. There, true to his word, are two crates stacked atop each other—identical, so far as I can tell, to the one my uncle had—both of them filled with pristine butterfly conch shells nestled in straw. Although their inner linings vary a bit from one to the next, they're all about the same size, and I'm struck again by how expensive they must be . . . how much care had to be put into selecting only the most showroom-ready specimens for shipment.

A new theory is beginning to form in my mind as I poke

around in the top crate, but Xavier grows antsy about having me in the employee-only area, so I take a few pictures with my phone and let him escort me out again. We say our goodbyes, and I head back along the pier in a daze, the sun glittering on the waves and making the stones of the jetty shine. I don't even wait until I'm on the sand before I'm scrolling through my photo gallery, examining the shots I took the previous afternoon—praying that I accidentally managed to capture a detail I didn't know I'd need later.

A crate of seashells wasn't what I was looking for in my uncle's house, and I curse my lack of foresight for not being more careful about documenting the find. Swiping from one unusable picture to the next, pressure builds in my chest. I can't break in again now that it's the scene of a crime, and I don't think for a second that the sheriff will be in a mood to listen to more of my half-cocked theories. Especially when I don't even fully know what I'm thinking myself.

But then I freeze, mid-swipe, staring at one of the last photos I took of the crate in my uncle's living room . . . at something stamped on the side, just barely visible beside the mound of cast-off laundry. A serial number, the black ink crisp and mercifully legible. I enlarge it and check it against the ones I just snapped in the Whitecaps storeroom. My scalp prickles as I realize they form a clean sequence.

Flash's crate came from the exact same shipment as Vincent Webb's.

My bike is chained up outside the Beachcomber, and I barely slow down long enough to unlock it. Certain events are starting to become clearer to me, although I'm not sure I understand where the trail I've uncovered is leading. At a glance, it appears my uncle somehow came into possession of rare seashells that clearly belonged to Vincent Webb, and that he was selling them to tourists on the beach. As ideas go, it strikes me as quite self-evidently a bad one . . . but before I let the conclusions draw themselves, I need a little more information.

It's not even noon yet, but the Double Barrel crew is right where I saw them last: lined up at the bar. Although today's tipple of choice is cheap beer instead of cheap whiskey. When they see me, they let up a cheer.

"Freddie—we need a round for Sparks!" Gravy calls out to the far end of the counter, and the surly bartender offers only a one-fingered gesture in response.

"You could at least get him a soda," Carlos interjects. "The kid's dad just got arrested! Cut him some slack."

It's like déjà vu all over again, and it answers one of the questions I'd meant to ask. But still, I venture, "So I guess you guys already heard what happened last night."

"Yeah." Carlos looks down at the bar. "Think most of the town knows by now. Bad news travels fast. Sorry about . . . well, all of it. You're having a hell of a week."

"Nobody thinks Luke did it," Ziegler says, like he's daring someone to contradict him—which, ironically, makes it less comforting. "It's some kinda misunderstanding, and it'll all get cleared up. Just watch."

"There's a maniac on the loose." Spitfire has already had one too many. "We better keep our doors locked, because they're out there killing people!"

"Listen," I say to Gravy, because he seems slightly less inebriated than his compatriots. "That cargo job you guys all did on the docks in Franklin Harbor a few weeks back, the one Flash walked off on? Do you remember . . . ? Do you know what kind of cargo you guys were unloading?"

"Just stuff for Vincent Webb." Gravy makes a loose gesture. "We don't usually ask, and they don't usually tell us. Long as we get paid, that's what matters."

"Got it," I say, a little deflated. Pulling out my phone, I show him the pictures I took of the crates—both the ones from Whitecaps and the one from Flash's place. "Do these look like the crates they had you carrying?"

"Maybe?" He wrinkles his nose, turning the display so Ziegler and Carlos can see it. "I mean, how many different ways can a crate look, though, right? What's in 'em?"

"Seashells." I watch their expressions, but no light bulbs go on. Once again, it's Freddie, the bartender, who makes the connection.

"You mean like the ones he was selling on the beach?" He leans over and takes a look at my phone as well. "Is *that* where he got them?"

"I think so," I answer just as Ziegler starts to chuckle. The humor spreads to Carlos, and then Gravy and Spitfire, and they're all laughing openly as the phone is passed back into my hands. "What is it? What's so funny?"

"Of course that's where he got them." Ziegler guffaws. "I should've known he was up to something when he ducked out like that. I can't believe he didn't just say something!"

"Typical Flash." Carlos raises his beer to my uncle's memory. "Wanted to see how good the haul was before giving us a chance to ask for a cut. Damn, I'm really gonna miss that selfish SOB." Catching my expression, he leans in with a conspiratorial wink. "I don't mean to burst your bubble or nothin', but your uncle . . . well, sometimes cargo followed him home on days he worked the docks."

"You mean he stole stuff?" My brows go up.

"He wasn't a klepto or nothing," Ziegler adds righteously. "It was just like . . . you know, if there was a lot of stuff being moved, and we weren't supervised properly, every now and then he'd snag one of the smaller crates for himself. Take it home, sell whatever was inside for some extra cash."

"It was one of his side hustles." Gravy leans across and clinks his bottle to Ziegler's. "Remember the scented candles? Fifty packs of votives that smelled like pumpkin spice, and he was trying to move them on the beach over Labor Day weekend."

"He sold a few, too!" Spitfire recalls. "Not like the time he lifted that box full of 'I Burned My Butt in Baja' oven mitts. Those went right in the trash."

"Dude, remember the time he ended up with five hundred key chains that all said 'Nevaeh' on them? And he tried to sell them online, but it turned out the cost of postage was more than what he thought to charge in the first place?" Gravy laughs so hard there are tears streaming down his cheeks. "I've still got one hanging from my rearview mirror!"

Carlos finally seems to catch the look on my face, because he reaches over and thumps me on the back. "Hey, Sparks, don't judge the guy too harshly, okay? The pay on these jobs is crap, and when you're day labor, nobody foots the hospital bills if you get hurt. Flash was just . . . evening the playing field a little."

"He wasn't afraid of getting caught?" I ask next, still a little troubled—even though I knew my uncle well enough not to be too surprised by the revelations.

"Those key chains cost about forty cents to make, and they sell 'em for seven bucks," Gravy tells me. "They got theft and loss factored into the price already—I mean, you're paying for 'em whether they make it off the truck or not, so they're not calling the FBI over a crate they lost track of here or there. Plus, the shipments are insured. No rich guy lost his shirt because his Nevaeh key chains didn't show up, trust me."

"Flash had sticky fingers, but he never hurt nobody." Ziegler sighs. "I just don't know why he didn't tell us about it this time. He always told us afterward."

"Yeah, but he kinda disappeared afterward." Spitfire is drunk enough that he doesn't bother to hide the hurt in his voice. "Even when he pulled something he *could* sell—like those headphones, or the charger cables—he'd only drop off the radar for a few days. And then he'd roll in here, rich as Midas, and treat us all to a couple rounds."

Freddie snorts. "How much could he have even made off seashells? College kids save every dime they've got for beer money. Who's on the beach right now paying big for crap they can find on their own for free?"

I would tell him the shells in question were butterfly conchs, but his point would still stand. Collectors might be eager to lay their hands on them, and a handful of gullible vacationers could probably be talked into a sale, if the pitch was right . . . but two weeks after the Franklin Harbor job, the crate I saw at Flash's place was still mostly full. And Paige sure didn't act like she was handling something valuable when she hurled one at me in Dad's office. They couldn't have been earning much off that surprisingly precious haul.

So why *did* my uncle drop off the radar? At first, I thought maybe it was because he'd bitten off more than he could chew—that he'd opened the crate and realized that, for once, he'd stolen something that couldn't be missed or written off. If he was afraid someone would go looking for it, and he was the non-union guy who'd quit early the day it disappeared, I could understand why he'd lie low. If he'd walked off with a small fortune in merchandise belonging to Vincent Webb, it might even constitute a motive for murder that had nothing to do with Bel Mondo International.

But then . . . he didn't exactly lie low, either—he hawked the shells on the beach, in front of God and everybody, and apparently even got into a fight over them with a Spring Breaker. More to the point, no matter how much the finest conch might fetch at auction, no matter how much tourists might pay for them as "one-of-a-kind" souvenirs, Vincent Webb treats them like paperweights at Whitecaps. They're not being sold for profit or even acquired for private appreciation; according to Xavier, the restaurant doesn't even bat an eye if customers swipe them right off the tables. Somehow my uncle managed to steal something truly valuable and yet totally worthless at the same time.

And all of it just puts me right back at square one, and with no new answers—because I can't imagine Webb killing anyone over seashells he doesn't particularly care about. And even though I can't explain why Flash would hide the shells from his friends and lie to me about the fight he had with the Spring Breaker, those questions don't point me in any new directions. Unless I can somehow turn up new evidence, there's only one suspect on the board with unquestionable motive, means, and opportunity.

My dad.

# TWENTY-ONE

When I get back to the Beachcomber, my mood about as bad as it's ever been, I let myself into Dad's office and start calling all our employees to let them know we're staying open today. Two seasonal hires say they've decided not to come back—and while I can't exactly blame them, I can literally feel an ulcer starting to form in my gut at the same time. Any desire I had left to run this place someday evaporates on the spot.

The truth is, I don't really know *what* I want to do with my future, but right now, managing the Beachcomber, as important as it's been in my life, feels more like a burden than a privilege. Maybe college will change my mind about that, I don't know. But I don't want to feel like my only options are the Beachcomber or turning into one more

Barton Beach slacker, day-drinking at the Double Barrel.

I scan through what remains of the to-do list Dad was making before he got arrested. I need to figure out who's really behind the murders in Barton Beach for his sake so he can get back to doing what he loves—but also for my own sake as well. Because I don't feel any sense of joy or accomplishment thinking about the shoes I have to fill tonight. I want my family whole and happy . . . but I don't think I want to live my dad's dreams, and all I can do is hope he'll understand that.

---

The cooks show up for work first, followed by the remaining back-of-house staff, and then the servers who really need the tips they're going to earn tonight—provided that all the bad publicity doesn't chase the rest of our business away for good. In the midafternoon, Mrs. Hughes drops Ruby off so she can help with the prep, and then, shortly before we have to open for the late-lunch crowd, the temporary manager arrives from Whitecaps.

"Nelson," he says by way of introduction, shaking my hand with a paw the size of a catcher's mitt. He's tall, with a tidy mustache and a bull neck, and he scowls like he wishes he could be anywhere else right now.

"Thanks for coming down to help us." I force a weak smile. "It was really nice of—"

"I'm not here as a favor—I'm doing my job." He stops

me short, rolling up his sleeves as he looks around. Swollen with muscle, tattoos crawling up his arms under his black button-down, he looks more like a bodyguard than a shift manager. With a disdainful glance at the dining room, he adds, "Trust me, I wouldn't be here if I wasn't getting paid for it. From what I can see, I'm gonna have my work cut out for me."

"Um"—what the hell am I supposed to say to that?—"okay."

"You." He points at Mia, who's been wiping down the indoor tables. "You're not planning to wear that. You have something more appropriate you can change into?"

Mia straightens up, looking down at her clothes— shorts, a simple tee, her apron—and then folds her arms across her chest. "What's wrong with my clothes?"

"You look like what you're selling isn't on the menu," Nelson answers crudely, gesturing for the back of the restaurant. "Go put on something else."

"There is nothing wrong with my clothes, or with how much of my skin is showing." Mia keeps her tone level, but color rises in her cheeks. "I don't need to change just because you're a disgusting, misogynistic creep."

Nelson's face begins to turn purple, and before he can fire or drive off one of the few servers we've got left, I intervene. "What she's wearing is fine. This is the beach, okay? As long as they stay in the garden, we don't even make the customers put their shoes on."

Nelson shakes his head. "I guess that attitude explains why the place looks like this, then. 'No shirt, no shoes, no sense keeping anything clean'?"

"We clean every day." I step back, a little offended. "And you don't have to be—"

"You don't clean very thoroughly," he retorts, dragging his thumbnail along the grout of the front window frame, pulling it back to show me the dirt he picked up. "Is the kitchen this filthy, too?"

Without waiting for an answer, he shoves past me, striding for the door to the rear area. Looking around me, at a room full of stunned and disgruntled faces, I stammer an apology. "L-listen, I'm sorry about all this. It's just temporary, until Dad is cleared, and then everything will go back to normal. I'll talk to—Well, I'll get it sorted out."

The problem is, I don't really know how to sort this out. This restaurant might belong to my family, but I can already tell Nelson won't be answering to me. I'll feel pathetic calling Mr. Webb and telling him the employee he graciously loaned us is a total jerk and could he please instruct the guy to be nicer? But that may be what has to happen.

When I catch up with Nelson again, he's dressing down the cooks, yelling at them about how messy the line looks and how items aren't stacked properly in the cooler. He opens cupboards, complaining about how the dry goods are organized, how much dust is on the shelves, how much sand has blown in through the back exit. He nearly brings down the pot rack when he catches his shoulder on the rope that's barely holding it up, and then glares at us all in contempt.

The whole experience makes me more self-conscious than ever about how run-down things have gotten over the years, and when he starts going through the employee lockers, I finally decide I've had enough. "Wait, whoa, you can't do that!"

He has one of the doors open, his arm elbow deep in someone else's belongings, and when I slam it shut on him, I catch the business end of his anger. Turning on me, getting in my face, he snaps, "Don't tell me how to do my job, kid. If you want to take over tonight, be my guest, but if I'm the one running the show, then the show runs by my rules. Got it?"

"News flash, dude: This isn't Whitecaps!" My ears burn, but I won't back down. "All this stuff belongs to our employees, and they're entitled to their privacy! Anyway, what we need is a manager, not a building inspector. If you don't want to be here, I can call Mr. Webb and ask if he has anyone else—"

"He doesn't." Nelson opens the locker right back up again, defiantly searching through it while I stand helplessly by. "And you know what? A *good* manager pays attention to how his kitchen is being maintained and what his employees are up to. I mean, who do you even hire here? Students and ex-cons, and people trying to make a living off tips from drunk college kids?" He scoffs. "If you think they're not stealing from you, you're an idiot. A few random locker searches might hurt morale, but they'll save you a ton in lost revenue."

He finds nothing in the lockers, but it doesn't stop him from going out on the floor and delivering an insulting lecture to the servers that they'll be fired if he catches them eating anything from the kitchen without paying for it first. After that, he marches straight to my dad's office and lets himself inside, taking a seat behind the desk like he owns the place. Without even looking to see if I've followed him, he gestures to the safe. "What's the combination to that thing?"

A little warning bell finally starts to jingle in the back of my mind, and before answering, I hesitate just long enough to catch his attention. "I don't know."

"You're lying." He narrows his eyes, his thick brows coming together.

"I'm not." I spread my hands, palms to the ceiling. "I'm sixteen; you think my dad trusts me with the combination to the safe?"

It plays right into his clear prejudice against us—my family, the Beachcomber, everyone who works here—so he just watches me for a moment and then scowls. "How the hell am I supposed to do the job if I don't have access to petty cash? And what about the receipts at the end of the night?"

Giving him my most innocent look, I say, "I don't know, man, I'm just a busboy. You're pretty smart, though. I bet you'll come up with something."

Backing out of the office, I shut the door, and then I just stand behind the bar for a moment, my heart thumping so hard I can feel each beat twice. His belittling comments about the employees, his judgmental evaluation of our housekeeping, his startling rudeness . . . it was all an act calculated to distract me from what he was really doing. And it almost worked, too, because right before my eyes, he went through every cupboard and drawer he could find— and it wasn't until he was right where I saw Paige last, asking me the same thing she did, that I realized the truth.

*He was searching for something.*

As revelations go, it's kind of a game changer—but I don't have time to think about the ramifications, because the doors open at last, and the first wave of the midday rush is upon us. For the next couple hours, I'm run off my feet, scurrying back and forth from the outdoor tables to the kitchen and back again. The whole time, all I can think about is what Nelson is looking for—what Vincent Webb must have sent him to find.

I haven't had a chance to open the safe since Dad's arrest, so I've got no idea what's inside it—and now I'll probably have to leave it shut tight until I know I'm alone. *Did* Flash go into the office that night? It doesn't seem possible, but Paige was convinced that the butterfly conch was my uncle's calling card. And maybe it was. Only a short time before I ran into him, he'd been fighting under the pier over a seashell, and then he'd come into the Beachcomber in order to hide.

But what if he wasn't here to hide himself, but to hide *something else?*

"Uh, Zac?" One of the servers appears suddenly in front of me, and she doesn't look happy. "There's some kind of, uh . . . disturbance out front? And I think it's about your uncle?"

Confused, I walk out onto the beach . . . and right into the middle of some sort of altercation. Three Spring Breakers—the same "You must love getting to work on the beach" girls who were here the night Flash died—are getting in Mia's face, all yelling at once.

"He said he worked here!" one of the girls insists, her face the same bright pink as the sunburned skin across her shoulders. I can already smell the beer on her breath from here. "That makes you responsible!"

"We want our money back," the second girl demands, stepping closer.

"What's going on?" I ask, but no one so much as looks my way.

"Look, can you please just . . . not shout at me?" Mia is at the end of her patience. "If you bought something at the Beachcomber and you want to return it, you can take your receipt to the—"

"We just *told you* we bought it *on the beach*!" the third girl snarls, jostling even closer. "The dude didn't give us a receipt, okay? But we want our money back, and we are not going anywhere until we get it!"

"I don't know what to tell you." Mia throws her hands up. "We don't sell stuff 'on the beach'; we sell it inside—where the cash registers are—and they print receipts automatically."

"Okay, it sounds like maybe there was some kind of misunderstanding?" I make another attempt at intervening. "Just because he told you he worked here doesn't mean he was representing the restaurant—"

"*You're* trying to *gaslight* me!" the third girl yells in my face.

Curtly, Mia steps in. "Look, the point is that if you bought something off a random weirdo, then it doesn't actually matter what his day job is; it's got nothing to do with the Beachcomber."

"He didn't say he worked here." The second girl is more lucid than her companions. "He said this was his restaurant—like, that he's the owner. That means it actually *does* have something to do with you, you stuck-up b—"

"What's all this screaming about?" a voice bellows over my head, and we all freeze, turning to see Nelson stalking toward us. Immediately, the three girls turn away from Mia to present a united front against the new authority figure.

"We were here earlier this week," the second girl begins, her attitude as hostile as Nelson's own, "and this old surfer-looking dude on the beach sold us *these*." Reaching into her shoulder bag, she pulls out a butterfly conch—and by this point, I can't even pretend I'm surprised to see it. "He said they were super rare, and that they ordinarily cost, like hundreds of dollars—"

"He even showed us a website to prove it!" the third girl clamors to add. "It was, like, eBay for seashells, or some-thing, and people were literally bidding *hundreds* on these!"

"So we believed him, but it was a *lie*, and we want our money back!" The second girl jabs the shell into Nelson's chest again, and when he finally takes it, she reaches into her bag and pulls out a second one. "He said this was his restaurant, so don't give us all that 'nothing to do with us' crap. He owes us, and now we can't find him, so that means *you* owe us. Okay?"

Maybe I should just let this play out—let Nelson dis-cover just how much fun it is to work "on the beach" for a bit—but this is also my chance to get an answer to the question that's been bugging me for days. "Why was it a lie? Why do you want your money back?"

"Because." The first girl reaches into the second girl's bag and produces yet another shell, which she shoves into my hands. When I look down at it, my eyebrows rocket up into my hairline—and I know exactly what she's going to say before she says it. "It's a *fake*."

The shell in my hands is the right weight, the right texture . . . it feels 100 percent real. And yet. Right at the edge of the aperture, where the silky inner edge meets the outer lip, the delicate blue-and-banded pattern that makes this species so unique and so rare is chipped. And exposed beneath it is the soft peach surface of a common, ordinary conch shell instead.

It's painted. *It's fake.* A really good fake—the counterfeit surface laid down over an actual conch, so it's convincing to anyone who knows what a shell is supposed to look and feel like—but it's a fake nonetheless.

And just like that . . . everything clicks into place for me. And I finally get it. I finally understand why Flash was here the night he died, why Paige had those bruises on her throat, why that crate my uncle stole was completely worthless . . . and yet cost him his life in the end. In fact, I think I even know what Paige and Nelson were trying to find in the Beachcomber, and it won't be in my dad's safe.

*I get it.*

And when I look up—too soon, before I've managed

to erase the sudden shock of understanding from my expression—my eyes meet Nelson's . . . and my blood runs cold. Because, in that one fleeting instant, I watch in real time as he realizes that I've got everything figured out . . . and that he'll have to do something about it.

# TWENTY-TWO

Nelson's big mistake is trying to shrug off the trio of irate girls, to shut them down with what I've come to recognize as his trademark unfriendliness. But if I've learned anything about the kind of Spring Breakers we see on the beach, it's that when they get into "I want to speak to the manager" mode, rude rebuffs only make them more determined. Within seconds, they've got him surrounded, hammering complaints at him like they're being paid for it—and I'm able to slip away.

The problem is, I've got nowhere to slip. With each minute that passes, the Beachcomber only gets busier and more crowded, the dining room packed and the kitchen frantic with activity. I can't go where I want, to ascertain my theory, without being seen—and if Nelson learns where he should have been looking all this time, the game will be over, and we'll all lose. But I can't just duck out, either; if Ruby and I disappear, he'll make sure people search for us, and there's nowhere we can go he won't think to look.

Plus, I'm worried that he'll eventually find what he came to the Beachcomber for in the first place—and I'll need to stick around in order to head him off. I need to get to it first if I want Sheriff Seymour to believe the wild tale I'm going to spin in my dad's defense.

Inevitably, Nelson shakes off the Spring Breakers . . . but he doesn't attempt a confrontation. Instead, he fades into the background, watching me without seeming to watch me, and as the evening wears on, my skin begins to crawl with the awareness of him always somewhere over my shoulder. I know he can't risk accosting me in front of witnesses—and I dodge a few of the summons he issues for me to come see him in the office, the one place on the premises where there might be a little privacy. But the more time that passes without him making a point to find out what I know, the more I begin to question whether that moment between us out front really meant what I thought it did.

At the time, with the counterfeit shell in hand, it felt like my deductions were stamped over my expression as clearly as the serial numbers on Vincent Webb's crates. But maybe I'm being paranoid. As I'm carrying a tub of dirty dishes back to the kitchen, my eyes stray around the room, and I wonder if maybe I can risk doing a surreptitious little search of my own. But then my gaze lands on Ruby, who's watching me back with blatant curiosity, and I come to my senses again.

No matter what I do next, I can't risk making any move that might put Ruby in danger. Even if Nelson doesn't know what I've figured out, I can't do anything that might tip him off; I can't take the chance that he's not watching me, or having someone else keep tabs on me for him.

So I do my job—clearing tables, taking out the trash, sweeping up broken glass—and the whole time, I pretend not to be minding Nelson while he pretends not to be minding me. My feet are starting to hurt by the time the dinner rush dwindles, only the dedicated drinkers remaining in the bar and garden, and I do my best to suppress any emotion that isn't pure relief at having had a successful night for once.

The final hours before closing are a blur, and I make sure to keep Ruby and Mia close by as we clean up, Nelson brooding in silence as he totals the receipts. I still haven't given him the combination to the safe, which means he'll have to take everything straight to the bank and leave it in the night deposit box after we're done. And because I have the keys to the restaurant, he won't be able to get back in and search the place when it's empty.

But I will.

As we're snapping off the lights and doing our final walk-through, I'm aware that this is the moment he's most likely to make his move—to take me aside when I've run out of excuses to avoid him and issue his worst threats. If I'm right about my suspicions, he may already have been involved in three homicides so far, and I've no doubt that if I can't find the evidence to prove it tonight . . . I may be the next body washing up on Barton Beach.

To my surprise, however, Nelson says nothing to me. There's no face-off, no remarks with a double meaning, no request that I accompany him to the bank; he keeps his mouth shut, his jaw clenched so tight the muscles bulge in his neck, while I lock the doors. And then he stalks away into the night without so much as a goodbye. I should probably be relieved, and yet . . . something about his conspicuous silence leaves me unsettled. I feel his eyes on my back the whole way home.

Something nobody tells you when you're trying to solve a murder for which your father has been wrongly arrested: When it's smart to take people into your confidence, and when it's smarter to leave them out of it. Especially if you think the real killer might come after anyone who knows the truth. If I tell Mrs. Hughes, for example, she may not take me seriously, but she'll definitely stop me from going ahead with my plan;

if I tell Xavier, he'll tell his mom; and if I tell Ruby, she may rat me out if I don't let her come with me.

Maybe I *should* let an adult take over. Show Mrs. Hughes the photos that have me convinced I know what my uncle was hiding, give her the keys to the restaurant and let her and her husband go beat Nelson to the prize. They might even be willing to do it . . . if they don't just dismiss my theory as the paranoid fantasies of a desperate kid—the way the sheriff certainly would, given how badly I've compromised my reputation with her. But I can't forget the way Mr. Webb's right-hand man watched me tonight; how, without saying a word, he convinced me he knew I was up to something. I'd never forgive myself if I put my best friend's parents on his radar in my place, and something happened to them.

So, instead, I lie in the dark, staring at the ceiling, waiting until I think enough time has passed that everyone is asleep. And then I get dressed again, leaving a brief note behind on my pillow that explains where I've gone and why—just in case I never make it back again.

With luck, I'll have this wrapped up before anyone even knows I left in the first place, at which point I'll have all the proof I need to free my father and put the real killer behind bars. But if something goes wrong . . . well, I can't bear the thought of Ruby spending the rest of her life believing I "accidentally" drowned in the cove or got killed by junkies during a drug deal.

It's late enough that the beach is deserted when I get to the Beachcomber, my bike tires squeaking and chuffing against their chrome guard. The temperature has dropped, and it's cold enough that I can see my breath, puffs of steam feathering in the stark moonlight and then gone again. The boardwalk businesses are closed, and dark waves slap against the jetty, the beacon flashing a silent warning that won't do me any good.

It's not quiet out here. Between the crash of the ocean, the surge and froth of Dead Man's Cove, and the wind gusting down the coast and making tarpaulins flap across the fronts of shuttered food stalls, it's hard for me to listen for voices or footsteps in the dark. I don't see anyone, but still, I creep through the shadows under the boardwalk, making my way to the back of the restaurant with as much cover as possible, keeping my eyes peeled.

I glance at my phone one last time, examining my pictures from Flash and Paige's bungalow, telling myself I haven't completely lost it. It was a photo I took in their kitchen—a total afterthought, just an impulse to capture the overall disarray—that filled in that one last crucial blank. Or . . . at least I think it did. If I really am right, I'll know for certain in a few minutes.

When I'm as convinced as I can be that the coast is clear, I dart across the strip of sand between the boardwalk and the back of the restaurant—the last place I ever saw my uncle alive—and unlock the Beachcomber's kitchen door.

Paige was convinced my uncle had been inside the office—*Flash was here that night; you said so*—and that she'd find what she was looking for there. But that's not where I ran into him. And it's not where he would have gone first, anyway. If he had something dangerous enough in his possession that he wanted to hide it from everyone, including his wife, he wouldn't have put it somewhere he'd have known for sure my dad would find it.

The kitchen is so dark, I have to use my flashlight app to see as I pick my way to the walk-in freezer, which still hums quietly against the resounding emptiness of the restaurant. I've been in here after hours plenty of times, but never this late—never when I was my only company— and my nerves are worn thin. There's a sound, a faint clink, and I whip around with my heart in my throat . . . but I see nothing that doesn't belong. The sound doesn't come again, but I hold my breath until my lungs hurt, just listening for it.

Did Flash know he was going to die? Did Shotgun? I think Paige did, based on the way she looked when I last saw her—her pale face, the dark bruises, the way her hands shook when she smoked. She had to have known that if she couldn't find what she was looking for, her number was up.

Fluorescent bulbs blink to life inside the freezer, gleaming against plastic bags and metal shelving, and I kneel down beside the stack of frozen peas. Even at the time, his story struck me as odd—coming into the restaurant for something to ice his black eye, when he was specifically avoiding my dad. When there's an ice machine out front, and countless other places he could have gotten some up and down the beach.

I go through the bags of frozen peas carefully, feeling around behind them before moving on to the stacks of vegetables on either side. I check the shelf above, and then the shelf below, and my fingers are going numb by the time I find something that doesn't belong—a fat Ziploc bag wedged against the wall behind a mountain of sacks holding tiger prawns. It's been there so long, the plastic is stuck, and I have to finesse it loose with clumsy hands . . . but then I'm drawing it out into the light at last.

It turns out to be several bags—or maybe something wrapped in multiple layers of plastic, and then bagged. I can't even tell if it's pills or powder . . . but I don't need a hand-printed label to tell me what my uncle stashed in our walk-in. My memory echoes with what the deputies told me after Shotgun died: *Drug sales on the beach are about as common as seagulls come spring break.*

When I first realized he'd stolen the conch shells from Vincent Webb, I thought maybe that was why he'd been killed, but it didn't make any sense he would be in danger for taking and reselling something that was ultimately worthless.

*Unless counterfeit shells hadn't been the only things packed inside that crate.*

It had been that mess in the kitchen, including the bags of ground coffee sitting out on the counter, that finally made me see the light. They didn't strike me as particularly significant at the time, although it did seem like an awful lot for two people who didn't even own a pot to brew it in, and I didn't dwell on them much after I left. But it's an old smuggling trick—packing illicit goods with coffee, as a way to hide the scent signature and throw off police dogs. And it was the only logical explanation for what had been going on in Barton Beach, right under our noses.

Flash stole a random crate, hoping for something he could sell . . . and ended up with a shipment of drugs meant for Vincent Webb. Who knows what went through my uncle's head when he realized his mistake. He'd grabbed a tiger by the tail—and even if the tiger wasn't what he'd been after, he'd gotten hold of it by intentionally stealing from the most powerful man in town. Returning the parcel with a humble apology and a promise not to do it again wasn't going to cut it at that point, and he had to have recognized how dire the situation was.

Is that why he was suddenly so eager to sell the Beachcomber? And when Paige came in here, shaken and scared, urgently seeking the missing drugs, did she demand the buyout so she could pay Webb back, or so she could get out of town? When I saw those bruises on her throat, I'd thought maybe she'd gotten them from struggling with Shotgun under the boardwalk, but it was also two days after Webb's "sympathy" visit.

*I hope that one day you and Flash will be reunited, but in the meantime may this card keep his memory alive.* Recalling the man's choice of words sends chills up my spine as I realize the hidden meaning behind them. It was a warning, a message to Paige that she would share her husband's fate if she didn't find and return Webb's missing stash.

The same stash I currently hold in my frigid, trembling hands.

I'll have to turn it over to Sheriff Seymour—although I should probably show them to Mrs. Hughes, first, for a legal perspective. And, you know, an adult one. If this is how I'm going to exonerate my father, at the expense of the most connected man in town, I'm going to need people smarter than me to take over from here. A little voice warns that I'll be sorry . . . that the cops will claim the drugs being found at the Beachcomber only implicates Dad more. But it's the only chance I've got, so it's the one I'll have to take.

Tucking them under my arm, my whole body shivering from the cold, I duck back out of the freezer . . . and walk right into an ambush.

# TWENTY-THREE

"Evening, Zac." Vincent Webb is standing in the middle of the kitchen, a single light bulb switched on in a corner of the room, flinging distorted shadows across his face. Behind him, Nelson looms—and he's got a gun in his hand, pointed right at my chest. "Looks like you found something that belongs to me."

"Looks like you broke into my family's restaurant," I reply, my tongue sticking to the roof of my mouth. "So I guess maybe we're even."

He smiles, but it doesn't make him look any friendlier. "You got guts, I'll give you that. It's something I respect in a man . . . but not something I'm gonna have a lot of patience with tonight."

"You killed my uncle." The words sound so small and

thin, bouncing off all the tile and metal in the kitchen. I thought they'd have more impact.

"That's true." He tilts his head. "If it makes you feel any better, I didn't want to, but he didn't leave me much of a choice. I'm afraid your uncle wasn't a very honest guy."

"Unlike you?"

"I got business interests that don't always operate inside the law, let's say," he allows, splitting the finest of hairs, "but I always deal honestly with my customers and suppliers. I can be ruthless when I have to be, but that's not the same as being a thief."

"Interesting perspective." I inch a little bit to the side. "I look forward to your TED Talk."

They don't try to stop me from moving—presumably because there's nowhere for me to go. The back door is too far away for me to reach, even at a sprint, without Nelson getting a shot off, and they're standing between me and the pass-through to the dining room. So I take another step and watch the gun barrel shift with me.

"Truth is, Zac, I wasn't even planning to kill your uncle that night." Webb tucks his hands in his pockets, perfectly relaxed. "In a way, it was kind of an accident."

"You dragged him out on the jetty and threw him into the cove," I point out sharply. "How was that an 'accident'?"

"All he had to do was tell me where the product was— or, better yet, hand it over." Webb shakes his head sadly.

"But he got to thinking that it was his 'insurance policy,' or something. That I wouldn't mess with him as long as he was holding on to my merchandise."

"He was wrong." Nelson's interjection is cold and flat, and makes my stomach curdle.

"Well, like I said, I didn't mean to. At first." Webb gestures indifferently. "We took him out to the jetty to . . . persuade him a little. But he struggled, and there was a fight, and I guess Nelson hit Flash just a little too hard."

Nelson's expression remains deadpan. "Oops."

"At least your uncle had guts." Almost offhand, Webb adds, "It wasn't hard to figure out what had happened to my missing product, though. Flash had already started selling those shells on the beach before he even unpacked enough of that crate to find out what I was *really* importing. And I'd already reviewed the names of every person who worked the docks the day my cargo came in, so I knew he'd cut out early. Putting two and two together was almost too easy."

"He wouldn't give it back," Nelson adds.

The drugs weigh about eight hundred pounds under my arm. "Did you try saying 'please'?"

"Your uncle recognized the position he was in pretty quick. He knew I couldn't afford to overlook the problem, whether he handed it back or not. See, his coming across evidence of my . . . less-public business put me in a

vulnerable position—which he meant to take advantage of."
Webb's expression hardens.

I'm smart enough to read between those lines. "He blackmailed you?"

"More or less. He tried to ransom the product back to me," Webb clarifies, "which was also unacceptable. I guess he and his girlfriend needed a lot of money in a bad way."

"So his death wasn't really an accident after all, then, was it?" I return, inching a bit farther to the side. "You just killed him a few seconds earlier than you meant to."

"I guess you could say that."

"What about Shotgun? Was he an accident, too?" I dart a glance at the clock on the wall, but it's impossible to read in the shadows. Webb has barely moved, but I don't know how long he'll let me drag out this conversation. "And Paige?"

"Shotgun might as well have punched his own ticket. He was a loudmouth drunk with no imagination; he *really* tried to blackmail me." Webb rolls his eyes in disgust at the dead man's memory. "He was on the beach the night we had our little conversation with Flash . . . but then, I hear you're the one who turned that tidbit up for the sheriff."

"You know about that?" I go still.

"Course I do. It pays to keep my ear to the ground around here. I know way more than you think I do, Zac." The man smiles again, and it's the first time I think I've seen him look genuinely pleased. "Shotgun was gonna have to be dealt with sooner or later, but I'm afraid your nosing around meant it had to be sooner. He was a fool and an addict, and he wasn't gonna keep his mouth shut for long if the deputies put any pressure on him."

"When we learned he was being named a 'person of interest' in the investigation, we set up a meet with him under the boardwalk," Nelson chimes in. He's barely blinked since I've come out of the freezer, and I wonder if his gun arm is growing tired yet. "He thought he was finally cashing in, the idiot."

"And Paige?" I repeat, my voice even smaller. Neither of them has made a move to take the drugs from me yet, but they won't let me hold on to them indefinitely—and Webb, for all his talk of being an honest businessman, clearly has no problem taking lives.

"Once Flash was permanently out of the picture, I gave Paige a chance to find the package for me. She made it sound like she knew all your uncle's hidey-holes—and she was the one who told me you'd seen him here at the Beach-comber that night." Webb points at me, his fingers in the shape of a gun. "But when she couldn't find it, she started getting a little erratic. I heard that she tried to force Luke into buying her out of Flash's share of the restaurant, and when we caught up with her later that afternoon, she was packing a bag."

"She was planning to leave town?" The conclusion is

obvious enough, but the longer I keep them talking, the more time I've got to enact a brilliant escape.

"She knew her time was up." Nelson smirks with cold satisfaction. "We had a conversation that got . . . heated."

"Your father coming along right afterward was just his bad luck." Webb sighs. "I wasn't lying to you this morning, Zac. I really do have a ton of respect for him. He's done a lot to keep this place going, despite getting no help from his brother, and he fights hard on behalf of all the little guys in Barton Beach. I never wanted him mixed up in any of this."

"Well, you could always call Sheriff Seymour and explain," I remind him, taking one more sideways step. I've been inching away from the freezer and closer to the back door . . . but that isn't exactly where I've been headed, and I'm now within arm's reach of my intended destination. "I bet she'll be very understanding."

"I was trying to figure out how I could get someone into the Beachcomber long enough to really search the place," Webb continues, ignoring me. "Once Luke was arrested, I thought maybe you'd have to close down, and then we could stage a break-in. But that would've run the risk of a burglar alarm, or witnesses out for a moonlight stroll—and it wasn't until you came to see me about your father's bail money that the perfect opportunity fell right into my lap."

"And Mr. Personality over here fell right into mine." I

nod in Nelson's direction, using the motion as an excuse to sidle two more inches to my right.

"Since we're all being honest," the man returns, still holding the gun unnervingly steady, "I meant what I said, too. This place is a dump, and it's insulting that we have to let it dirty up the beach just to keep that damn resort from moving in."

"Bel Mondo building a hotel along the boardwalk would completely change the economy around here." Webb's eyes glint in the weird, sideways light. "Yeah, there would be more rich tourists spending their money, raising property values and causing small businesses—like yours—to go under. That's all true. But I'm not really as worried as I pretended to be; even if I have to close one of my motels, Whitecaps and my other businesses would survive." The man gestures at the bundle under my arm, just to let me know he hasn't forgotten about it. "Fact is, I make most of my money moving the kind of product your uncle found in that crate of conch shells he stole. A resort would mean a higher class of tourist, and increased pressure on local law enforcement to shut down the current drug trade in Barton Beach."

"Oh no, not that," I say, rolling my eyes theatrically. I'm one step away from my last chance to turn the tables, and I can sense my time running out. "How will we survive without the drug trade?"

"We wouldn't be without it. If anything, it would just get worse." Water drips somewhere in the darkness—a broken pipe, probably. One more thing to fix. "Resorts aren't for nuns, Zac. Not only will wealthy vacationers have great big drug problems, and lots of cash to invest in them, but they'll also be in way less danger of prosecution. The demand for cocaine and opioids will skyrocket, but they'll be bought and sold on newer, private networks that won't be easy to touch."

"So . . . your real goal is to keep the drug market in Barton Beach from being gentrified?" I remark. "How noble."

"It doesn't have to be noble—it just has to *be*. It's my goal, and I'll see that it's done." His eyes glint again, his back straightens . . . and I realize that this is it. *This is it.* "I told you before that I can be ruthless when it's necessary, and when it comes to protecting my empire, everything I've built and worked for, it usually is. Now"—he shoots his cuffs and then folds his hands in front of him—"be a good boy and give Nelson that package. We've gone to a lot of trouble to get it back, and I'm tired of waiting."

"Or you'll shoot me?" I wonder if they can even hear me over the thundering of my heart. "How are you going to convince the sheriff my father did it this time? He teleported to the restaurant, shot me for no reason with a disappearing gun, and then teleported back to jail?"

"What's going to happen is that you're going to give

that package to Nelson, and then we're all heading out to the jetty together, where you're gonna succumb to your despair over recent events at Dead Man's Cove." Webb's tone is casual, conversational, and it gives my nightmares the heebie-jeebies. "It'd be nice if you walked there with us under your own power, but it's not a requirement."

"So you're not going to shoot me," I summarize, a little relieved, taking one more step closer to the exit.

"A gun is good for other things, too, kid." Nelson starts forward, murder in his eyes. "For example, it's heavy enough to crack your skull open without killing you right away. I practiced that move on Paige when—"

He doesn't get to finish. Lunging to the side, I grab the rope that's been all that's kept our rickety pot rack aloft for the past few months and yank it free from its moorings. There's a clatter and a whoosh, the whole apparatus unbalancing . . . and then it drops with the force and speed of a meteor—an earsplitting tumult of steel and chrome and aluminum ripping free of the ceiling beams and crashing down on top of Nelson and Webb.

I don't wait to see how successful my impromptu booby trap was. Before the cascade of cookware has even settled, the air still ringing with the fury of tumbling metal, I take off like a shot—slamming through the back door and out into the night.

Sand churns under my feet as I race alongside the forest of

pilings in back of the Beachcomber. I need my bike, but I left it up on the boardwalk—near the phone store—so that I could make a stealthier approach through the shadows. A worthless plan that didn't account for Nelson and Webb anticipating my late-night return, and one that now leaves me breathless and panicked, afraid of what's over my shoulder.

I'm pretty sure Nelson is down for the count, the memory of him crumpling under the impact of the falling pots and pans playing over and over in my mind. But I didn't see what happened to Webb . . . and it's not like I've got much lead time, either way. There's only a few places I can go right now—home, the Hugheses' house, or the sheriff's station—and as soon as they come to, they'll be calling on reinforcements to intercept me.

The jetty's elevated walkway comes into view ahead of me, its irregular stones gleaming dully in the moonlight, stretching across the beach and out into the wind-tossed ocean. The beacon flashes, and waves slam hard into the cove, sending icy froth spraying into the night air. Pouring on speed, I make for the staircase that will lead me to where I left my bike. I've got the bag of drugs clamped so tightly under my arm that my shoulder is starting to cramp, and nervous sweat stings my eyes as it rolls from my hairline.

I'm ten feet from the stairs when the rear door to the Beachcomber slams open again and a gunshot explodes into the darkness at my back. *"STOP!"*

Adrenaline floods my system, my heart lurching, and a surge of dizzying fear nearly takes me off my feet. I stumble to a halt, waiting to feel the pain of a bullet . . . but it doesn't come. Heavy steps pound the sand behind me, and I make an uncoordinated turn to see Vincent Webb running at me through the shadows behind the beachfront businesses—his face bloodied and etched with rage, Nelson's gun outstretched in his white-knuckled grip.

"Stay right where you are, you little punk, or I'll put the next bullet through your head!" His teeth are bared, and I know he means it, but he's limping and he's still a good ten yards away.

Spinning back around, I take two steps for the staircase—and a second shot rings out, a bullet thunking into the piling right beside me. With a startled yelp, I jerk the other way, losing my balance in the shifting sand and sprawling to the ground. I'm just scrambling to my hands and knees again, grabbing for the plastic bag, when Webb catches up with me.

Sinking his fingers into my hair, he grabs an agonizing handful and yanks my head back, dragging me upright as he presses the barrel of the gun under my chin. "Nice and slow, Zac. Don't make me get your brains all over my shirt—it's Italian."

"P-please . . ." I wish I could say I was still brave, even with a gun digging into my flesh, but my teeth are chattering so badly it's hard to speak. "J-just take the drugs and let me go, okay? I won't tell anyone—"

"Oh, I'll take them," he snarls, his breath hot against my face. "But I think you'll understand if I don't exactly trust you to keep your mouth shut, yeah? I'm sorry, kid, but you haven't left me a lot of choices, here. Get on your feet— we're going for a walk."

He shoves me toward the path to the jetty, snatching the bagged drugs up from the sand and tucking them under his arm. My vision is clouded—with tears, with sweat, with terror—and I cast a hopeless glance back up at the boardwalk, willing someone to walk by. Willing someone to have heard the gunshots, to have called the sheriff. "You . . . you're not going to get away with this."

"Sure I am." Webb sticks the gun into my ribs this time, jabbing me hard enough to cause a bruise—not that I'll have long to worry about it. "Look at everything I've gotten away with so far! Now, let's move."

Pushing me ahead of him, steering me with a hand at the nape of my neck, he leaves me no opportunity to fight back—to turn the tables. The wind grows stronger the closer we get to the beacon, my feet sliding over damp stones, waves crashing into the jetty and spraying us both with frigid water. To one side, the ocean rocks in the moonlight, and to the other, the cove roils like a cauldron at a high boil. Everywhere the gun touches, I imagine a bullet ripping me open, tunneling through muscle and bone, tearing my life away. It can't end like this. It just can't.

"People will know what happened," I gasp out, struggling to maintain my balance as he propels me toward the literal end of the line. The moon shimmers on the horizon, and I try not to think about Flash, to imagine how he felt when Webb and Nelson were forcing him to make this exact same one-way trip. "I left a note explaining everything—about the conch shells and the drugs, and Nelson and *you* . . . if I die tonight, they're going to know you had something to do with it!"

"You mean you left a note full of wild and unsubstantiated theories." Webb grunts in my ear, the wind howling louder. "It means squat without proof—just a bunch of half-cocked speculation—and thanks to you, I got my hands on the only evidence that might possibly incriminate me. Without the drugs, all the cops have is a crate full of decorative novelties your uncle stole. And if that's what I was willing to kill over, I wouldn't have left it behind in the bungalow when I killed Paige, would I?" Triumphantly, he concludes, "Besides, you're something of the boy who cried wolf. Maybe the whole reason you're going to throw yourself into the cove tonight is to draw suspicion away from your father."

"You're a psychopath." As insults go, I don't think it hurts his feelings too much, because he laughs at me.

When we reach the beacon, the ocean slapping fiercely against the rocks, he shoves me so hard I fall to my knees. Struggling up again, I turn around, facing him. The beach stretches out at his back, lights glowing along the board-walk, reflecting in the surf. I've never seen our town from out here at night before; it's beautiful. As last sights go, I could do worse—I only wish I could enjoy it.

"Jump into the cove," Webb commands, still clutching the parcel under one arm.

I lick my lips, tasting salt. "If you shoot me, they'll know despair had nothing to do with my death. They'll know it was murder, and they'll come for you, for sure."

"If they try, I'll see to it that the sheriff loses her job." He grins, maniacal, his teeth gleaming in the flash of the bea-con. "I'll hire a world-class attorney, who will convince the public that a man who gives money to literacy programs and Meals on Wheels couldn't possibly be a murderer. And without any evidence, they'll eventually drop the charges anyway." Gesturing back at Barton Beach, he says, "Do you think your death'll be the first crime they've tried to pin on me? I've gotten away with more than you could ever dream of, Zac, and I'll get away with this, too. Now, jump—I'm all out of patience tonight."

The ocean surges, froth vaulting up my back, and I choke on my own heartbeat. For all my smart rhetoric, it won't make any difference if he gets caught for my murder or not—I'll still be dead. And without anyone left to corroborate the existence of the drugs, he just might get away with it after all. I could try to dive into the calmer waters to the north of the jetty, but he'd shoot me the second I moved in that direction . . . and even if he missed, he'd beat me back to the shore on foot.

"Your time is up, Zac." Webb racks the slide, stepping forward—but when the shot comes, I'm still taken by surprise.

There's a popping sound and then a loud crack as a bullet strikes the beacon, sending up a shower of broken concrete. I stumble back, my body filled with cold fire, a second shot ringing out across the water before I realize it's coming from the shore—not from in front of me. Webb twists instinctively, swinging the gun toward the coastline . . . and his fancy shoes lose purchase on the uneven stones. Slippery with froth and festooned with rotting kelp, they offer no traction as he unbalances, tottering sideways.

The gun goes off, a bullet slamming into the water, and I witness the moment he realizes he's going to fall—when his eyes pop wide and he lets go of the drugs, tossing his arms out for leverage. But he's too late. The waves leap, and he tumbles into their arms, a strangled howl following him beneath the surface of Dead Man's Cove. It's so dark, I lose sight of him in seconds . . . but not before I see his body slammed against one of the many jagged rocks that give the inlet its name.

He's pulled under, deeper, the relentless chop forcing him toward the shore, where the remnants of Flash's memorial still stand. Blood fills the water where he vanished from sight—or maybe that's just my imagination. Maybe it's a trick of the moon.

All I know for certain is that Vincent Webb is dead.

# EPILOGUE

"You must love getting to work on the beach!"

The woman who says it today is older, a retiree who's dropped by for an alfresco lunch with her husband, the pair of them watching the sun beat down on the sand from a table in the garden. The Spring Breakers have taken over the sand today, seizing advantage of a mini heat wave that's called them to enjoy the water. Beyond the shallows, where the swells are breaking into crests of foam, figures in wet suits ride the waves.

It's a nice enough day that I manage to not laugh right in their faces. "Most of the time, it's great."

I don't let them ask me about the other part of the time, because they're not prepared for the answer. Instead, I quickly clear off the table beside them and then hurry back to the kitchen with my bounty of dirty dishes. It's still a total mess in there one week later. The wreckage of the fallen pot rack has been cleared away, of course, but there's a hole in the ceiling where its one remaining mount was still bolted in place. The cookware that used to dangle overhead has since been moved to a rolling rack—which we have no room for and which migrates constantly as people try to get it out of their way.

Unable to resist, I look to the spot on the floor where Nelson had been buried under the debris, knocked out cold by the impact. Having broken his arm and gotten a concussion, he was still lying there when I led the cops to the restaurant after staggering back off the jetty and onto the beach that night.

"Ugh, I know that look on your face." Ruby glares at me from her usual chair. "You're trying to think of a new way you can brag to Mia about almost caving in the restaurant."

"I did not 'almost cave in' the restaurant!" I protest with a laugh—although it must be said that I did not exactly take into consideration the overall effect that dropping the pot rack would have on the ceiling supports at the time. "And I haven't been bragging, either. I just . . . you know, told her the story."

"Four different times," my sister points out dryly. "Just ask her out already."

"She'd only say no." With a sigh, I rub my face. "I literally brought down a murdering kingpin, single-handedly, and I still don't have a shot with Mia."

"Well, ask her out so she can turn you down and you can stop moping about it." Ruby has no patience for my lovesick misery. "And you weren't exactly single-handed, either. How come you never told her that I'm the reason the sheriff got there in time to save your butt from being killed by Vincent Webb?"

"Because you've already told her that—*five* times," I return—and if I didn't owe her a debt of gratitude, I'd be more annoyed. It's hard to look dashing in front of the girl I like when my coolest story ends with "And if it weren't for my twelve-year-old sister waking up early, finding the note I left on my pillow, and dialing 911, I'd be dead right now."

But it's true. Sheriff Seymour was just arriving at the far end of the beach, responding to Ruby's panicked call, when she heard Webb shooting at me. She caught sight of us as he forced me out onto the jetty in that final death march, and was just barely able to get into position in time to fire her pistol at the beacon. It was meant to be a warning, but it proved fatal enough in the end.

Ruby opens her mouth to make another comment, but right then, Mia herself barges into the kitchen. "There you guys are! You're wanted in the office. I guess the, uh . . . the sheriff is here?"

My sister and I exchange a glance and then get up at the

same time. Even though I'm not expecting any bad news, my track record with visits from law enforcement hasn't been so great these days, and my hands are tucked into nervous fists.

As we follow Mia out into the dining room, though, my steps falter a little. The light coming through the front windows makes her hair shine, and when she tosses it over her shoulder, I swallow audibly. As much as I hate to give my sister any credit, she kind of had a point just a minute ago. "Uh, Ruby, you can go on ahead—I'm right behind you, okay?"

"What do you mean? Why?" Then she sees where my attention is fixed and rolls her eyes behind her glasses. "Oh, good grief."

Thankfully, she doesn't argue, and once she's on her way, I summon up the courage to stop Mia just before she heads into the garden. "Hey, wait! I've been meaning to talk to you about something."

"Oh?" Her brow arches in a question—but she smiles, and it's brighter than the sunshine off the waves.

Melting inside a little, I open my mouth . . . but all my words vanish in a terrifying instant. My underarms get hot, my neck itches, and I look down at the floor. How is it possible that I could face down a gun and keep my wits together, but I can't ask Mia Montes on a date without turning into a nervous, stammering wreck?

*"Willyougooutwithme?"* I finally blurt, my face blazing. And even though it feels like I'm about to hit the downward slope of a roller coaster, I'm honestly just relieved that the words are out in the open. "I know you said I'm too young for you, but you're only, like, two years older than me—and how many guys do you know who've single-handedly brought down a drug kingpin?" I do not feel the least bit guilty for leaving Ruby out this time. "I think that kinda proves how mature I am, right?"

"It's three years," she points out—but, I notice with encouragement, she's still smiling. "And it's not about maturity. I like you a lot, but . . ." Mia shrugs again, her shoulders perfectly bronzed and perfectly shaped. "We're at totally different places in life right now. You're still in high school, and not only do I have no idea what I'm doing with my life, I don't even live in town! And you don't have a car."

"I have a bike?" Unfortunately, this sounds just as pathetic out loud as it did in my head. "Who cares, anyway? We still see each other, like, four nights a week."

"At work." Her tone is gentle but firm. "It's not the same thing."

"But it could be," I suggest weakly.

Mia touches my elbow, and warmth spreads all the way up my arm and into my brain. "It wouldn't be a good idea. There may only be three years between us, but they're pretty important ones, you know?"

"Yeah, I get it." My heart retreats from my throat, dropping all the way down into my stomach.

"I'm not opposed to being closer, though. As friends, I mean," she adds quickly. "We could get coffee before work, sometime. Or split some gross beach food on the boardwalk."

I give a mechanical nod, trying not to feel too dispirited. Being Mia's friend is better than just being her coworker, and who knows? Maybe I'll continue to grow on her. But, if I've learned anything from all this, it's that you have to shoot your shot while you still can.

"Coffee!" I call as she turns to walk away. My voice cracks, but I don't even care. "Next Wednesday?"

Mia throws her head back and laughs, and the sound is magical. "You're on." Then she steps in, pressing her lips to my cheek, filling me with the warm scent of strawberries and vanilla. My head spins, and my feet practically leave the floor as she pulls back again and heads toward her tables.

I float all the way to Dad's office. When I arrive, I find Sheriff Seymour perched on the edge of the desk. She smiles when she sees me come in. "Oh, good, you're here. I was about to update your father on the case."

"My favorite subject," Dad mutters, the air in the room a little too thick for comfortable breathing. Even though he was released the day after Vincent Webb died in the cove, the charges against him formally dropped, his relationship with the sheriff is way less congenial than it used to be.

Actually, a lot of things about Dad aren't like they used to be. It turns out that losing his brother, learning the most successful businessman in town was a demented criminal, and almost being put on trial for a triple homicide he didn't commit have affected his outlook. He buried himself back in work pretty much the instant he got released, but he has a far less rosy view of Barton Beach than before. I even think he finally understands why I might not want to "work on the beach" for the rest of my life.

"To begin with, they're putting the investigation of Webb's drug network into the hands of the Feds," Seymour reports, ignoring the tension in the room. "We expected as much, since it involves multiple jurisdictions, but it's still a little disappointing. I know you'll understand when I say that this particular case is personal. No matter where the shipments came from, or how many laws he broke transporting them, he was selling them in our community, damn it."

"I'm glad he's dead." Dad says this with no particular inflection—just a statement of fact. "At least there's no chance of him escaping justice on a technicality."

"Well, the murders are still ours to pursue." Sheriff Seymour adjusts her posture. "We may not be able to hold him accountable for them either, exactly, but we can nail them to his memory. His underlings have no reason to shield him anymore, and . . . well, they no longer have him to pay for their attorneys, either. Nelson Cargill, in particular, has been extremely cooperative."

"I'll bet he has." I press my lips together. "I mean, he's got the most to lose, right?"

"You could say that," the sheriff acknowledges. "He was Webb's right hand, and he admits to doing all the killings at his employer's behest—which matches your own account." Delicately, she continues, "He probably would have killed you as well, if you hadn't gotten the drop on him. So to speak."

I can't help it—I grin to myself, still a little smug about that move with the pot rack. If Webb had been standing one foot closer to his henchman, I'd have taken them both down, and I wouldn't have to put a Ruby-shaped asterisk at the end of my coolest story.

"So what happens now?" Dad asks, letting out a weary breath. "With Webb gone, and his empire crumbling, it'll probably devastate the town, won't it?"

"Maybe." The sheriff seems resigned. "Most of his assets have been seized, and those Bel Mondo people are wasting no time pressing their advantage in the face of all the bad publicity. Barton Beach is desperate for a win, and the hotel group is offering one up on a silver platter."

"A silver platter or a Venus flytrap?" Dad snorts.

Seymour sidesteps the embittered question. "What happens now for you?"

"I don't know." Dad looks around the room—at the water damage, the old carpet, the peeling caulk—and he shakes his head. "The truth is, I used to feel such a responsibility to this place. Now, though . . . I don't know. My brother never helped me run the Beachcomber, but it always felt like a family business, anyway. And that's how our dad always wanted it. But with him gone . . . it's just not the same." A mirthless smile turns up one corner of his mouth. "Plus, I don't know if you heard, but my son was almost murdered here recently."

This is something he has not let me forget, although he doesn't seem to have settled on an appropriate way to deal with it. He was furious that I kept up my investigation, terrified in retrospect by how close I came to losing my life—and he blew a gasket when he learned how much it would cost to fix the ceiling. But he also can't argue with the fact that I solved Uncle Flash's murder and saved him from wrongful arrest.

"What are you saying, Dad?" Ruby asks, her expression serious.

"I don't know," he repeats, but he smiles at us—and it's an affectionate one this time. "Maybe we should talk about it, as a family. The sheriff wasn't kidding when she said Bel Mondo is pressing their advantage; they've upped their offer on the Beachcomber, and at this point, it's a little hard to just dismiss out of hand."

"Are you saying you want to sell now?" I sit up straighter. This is what I wanted all along, I think . . . and yet now I don't know how to feel about it. Suddenly, it's too big for me to wrap my brain around.

If you'd asked me a month ago whether I could solve a multiple homicide or square off against an armed criminal and live to tell the tale, I'd have laughed in your face. But the events of this spring break have shown me I'm capable of way more than I ever thought. And in a strange, twisted way, it's taught me that maybe I *do* care about this sleepy little beach town after all. It always seemed like there were only two paths I could follow if I stayed here—Dad's or Flash's—but now, I'm starting to realize I might be able to forge one of my own.

"I'm saying I think we should talk about it," Dad says. Shoving his papers aside, he gets to his feet. "In fact, why don't we take the day off—the three of us? The restaurant won't collapse if we close for one more night." Then, laughing, "Well, maybe it will. But at least it won't collapse with us inside it."

Ruby and I exchange a glance, like, *Who is this man, and what did he do with our father?* "Are you sure?"

"Yeah. In fact, why don't we drive down to Spivey Point?" he suggests. "We can swing by the house and grab our wet suits . . . maybe we can paddle out for your uncle. It's how he'd have wanted us to honor his life."

Just like that, tears spring to my eyes. When Flash died, things fell apart so fast that we never got to have a memorial—we never got to sit around and remember him as a family—and I didn't realize how badly I needed it until now. "Wh-what about Ruby? The waves are pretty rough at Spivey; she might not be ready."

"I'll sit on the beach and make fun of you when you fall off your board," my sister decides. "That's how Uncle Flash would have wanted me to honor his life."

"Let's go break the news to the rest of the staff," Dad says, getting to his feet.

We say goodbye to the sheriff, and as we leave the office, I take one last look out the window—at the sun shining on the boardwalk, and the gulls wheeling in the sky. Maybe the future in Barton Beach won't be so bad after all.

# ABOUT HUNT A KILLER

Since 2016, Hunt A Killer has disrupted conventional forms of storytelling by delivering physical items, documents, and puzzles to tell immersive stories that bring friends and families together. What started as an in-person event has now grown into a thriving entertainment company with more than 100,000 subscribers and over four million boxes shipped. Hunt A Killer creates shared experiences and community for those seeking unique ways to socialize and challenge themselves.

# ABOUT THE AUTHOR

Photo credit: Uldis Balodis

**Caleb Roehrig** is a former actor and television producer who cannot seem to live in one place. Currently dividing his time between Chicago and Helsinki, Finland, he is an expert at writing on planes and recovering from jet lag. His young adult titles include the acclaimed thrillers *Last Seen Leaving, The Fell of Dark,* and *Death Prefers Blondes,* as well as *The Poison Pen*—a tie-in to the CW's popular *Riverdale* television series—and the Archie Horror original novel *A Werewolf in Riverdale.* His short stories have appeared in anthologies such as *His Hideous Heart, Out Now,* and *Serendipity.* Wherever he's living at the moment, he's there with his husband and an overabundance of books.